✑ JESUS ✑
The Egypt Years

GW01454269

❧ JESUS ☙
The Egypt Years

Femi Martin

Copyright © Femi Martin 2023

All places and characters in this story are solely imaginary.
Although the story is about real places and real people in real time.
The whole content of the story is solely the author's imagination
and it's written to give glory to God.

All rights reserved.

With all rights under the copyright reserved. No part of this book
may be reproduced, stored or introduce into a retrieval system or transmitted
in any form and by any means (electronic, mechanical, photocopying, recording
or otherwise,) without prior written permission of the copyright owner.

Coverpage design by Candice Broersma designs for Author
Edited by Elizabeth Smith
Typeset by Iram Allam
Development Editing by Oksana Marafioti
Proofread by Sugandha Gupta

First published online by Femi Martin 2023

For my mother

CRD Chapter 1 CRD

ARRIVING IN EGYPT

We've got to answer one question, and the question is, why doesn't the holy family settle down in one place in Egypt? As we know Egypt is a different country where King Herod has no power. But they travel down the coast to the south. They arrive at the time, in Pelusium in the night without any money or property, just the clothes they're wearing. And the presents the three wise men gave to baby Jesus.

Pelusium at that time is a bustling city with daily trades flowing through its large port. At night, the city takes to the inns that remain open. When ships dock at the port, shipmates and traders need accommodations, this keeps the city open through the night. Pelusium is the largest city outside Jerusalem and is close to Israel, so it houses many Jews who live in Egypt.

Entering the city at night, Joseph walks the donkey that Mary and baby Jesus are riding. Mary is breastfeeding baby Jesus as they go along. She worries about leaving Bethlehem in haste and making the journey. She feels sad and a tear falls from her eyes. She wipes it off with her headscarf then sees houses before her, instead of the desert land they've been travelling through. She calls to Joseph realizing that they've finally entered Egypt.

"Where will we stay for the night?" she asks. Her weariness

from the journey shows on her while she tries to concentrate on feeding baby Jesus.

"Let's go into the inn there," Joseph replies, pointing to an inn on the road.

He knows Mary has seen the inn before she asked. Joseph is still worried, even near to paranoia, about the new baby. Even the woman he's married to worries him. If not for the warning from the angel of God, he would have divorced Mary.

"We might find a bed there," he says.

"We have no money, Joseph," says Mary.

Joseph stops the donkey and looks into the bag containing the presents the three wise men gave to baby Jesus. He takes out the frankincense.

"This should pay for our stay."

When the innkeeper sees that they have a baby with them, he takes compassion on them, especially when Joseph says they've been travelling all day with the baby. He looks at the frankincense and sees that it's of superior quality. He's instantly amazed.

"Where did you get this?" he asks as suspicion grows in his voice.

"It's a present given to our baby when he was born. Since we have no use for it, can we trade it in for a room and some food?" Joseph says as he senses suspicion.

Cocking his head to the side, the innkeeper looks them up and down. Mary gets down from the donkey and comes closer, bringing her baby into view. Seeing the baby, the inn keeper goes in and comes out with drinks for them. He invites them inside and signs them in.

"My name is Al Hamond Gosham. You can call me Gosham. Everybody does," he says seeming overjoyed by something. "Stay as long as you want," he adds while giving them a key.

He keeps bowing his head down to the baby as they walk away to their room. Before they're settled in their room, food and clothing arrives from Gosham. They learn they've been given one of the best rooms at the inn. Mary gives baby Jesus a bath while Joseph goes into the city.

Coming into the city, he sees the port still busy and shipmates unloading their boats. He walks by the harbour and arrives at the port. Joseph is a carpenter, trained for in Galilee, but on this occasion he's open to any job on offer.

As he walks, Joseph is pondering on the angel's message that Herod sought to kill the baby. He believes it will only be in Bethlehem, being the place where baby Jesus was born. However, upon reaching the port a surprise awaits him. They did travel by land but to his surprise he's seeing Jewish people arrive by boat in hundreds. He's surprised and baffled at the same time, so he wants to learn more. He walks close to a family. The mother seems to be in tears and the rest of the family sombre.

"Hello, friends." Joseph says. The father stops and yells at Joseph.

"Can't you see we're in sorrow?"

"I'm sorry." Joseph says. "But why are you in sorrow?"

"It's Herod," the man continues. "He has gone mad. He's killing all the male children in Bethlehem. He killed my son. He was only a year old." He burst into tears.

Joseph immediately hugs the man. He feels sad for their loss knowing at once that he and Mary only might have missed Herod's men by a few seconds. That's the reason, the angel of the Lord had sent them out into Egypt in the middle of the night.

He grows fearful, knowing the extent of the damage Herod has caused just to kill baby Jesus. He allows the family to go while he walks down into the port. He meets more Jewish people bearing the same horrible story of King Herod's massacre. When

3

he reaches the harbour, he tells a foreman there that he needs a job to take care of his family.

"What can you do?" the foreman asks.

"I'm a carpenter by trade," Joseph says. "Right now, I will do anything."

"Good," the foreman says. "It just happens that we need some carpentry done on the boats. Come with me."

He takes Joseph into a boat and hands him a set of tools before he shows him damaged places around the boat that he wants fixed. For the past three months they've been traveling, Joseph had taken time to think about why Herod wants baby Jesus dead. Of course, he believes the angel of the Lord, but as a human he wonders anyway. He'd not imagined something this big. He never thought King Herod will go to such extreme lengths to have baby Jesus killed.

Joseph thinks about what he'd just heard. Although he wants to run back to the inn, and pack and leave the city with baby Jesus, yet he stays, knowing they will need every penny he can make. What frightens Joseph most is the fact that their enemy is King Herod, and in his fear, he forgets that God is greater than the king.

The room on the boat where the crew eats is in a big mess with most of the desks and benches broken. Joseph begins to fix them, seizing the opportunity to associate with the boat crews.

At the end of the night when Joseph returns to the inn, Mary is asleep while baby Jesus lies in a cot beside the bed. Joseph sees that the innkeeper has supplied everything they need. But he doesn't want to take advantage of the situation because he doesn't know how much a frankincense is worth. He doesn't know how long or how far the reach of the inn keeper's hospitality will go, so he wants to be cautious.

Joseph had decided to marry Mary when she was pregnant knowing that the baby is not his. He knows that he has taken on a great responsibility to act as earthly father to Jesus. He eats and falls into bed beside his wife till the break of dawn when Mary awakes.

Mary wakes up to baby Jesus's soft cries. She knows he's hungry and prepares for his breakfast. She sees Joseph still fast asleep and wonders what he was up to when he went out last night. She continues to care for her baby. By noon when Joseph wakes up, she gets to hear everything. She's playing with baby Jesus with a soft toy when Joseph wakes up.

"Mary, you have to hear what I heard at the port yesterday," he says.

Then he tells her about the families coming into Egypt from Bethlehem and what news they brought with them.

"That's why I know that God is with us," he says. "His angel told me to go into Egypt because Herod seeks to kill the child. How were we to know that King Herod will go this mad? It's crazy, a complete madness, killing all these children just to get to your son."

"What about his spies?" Mary says. She's quickly thinking ahead now that she knows. "He has spies everywhere. They will talk to him if they see us."

Joseph knows she's right. King Herod has spies everywhere and he pays them well enough for them to tell him anything they see. In the meantime, he thinks they should be safe where they are. He doesn't want to run again and since he hasn't heard from an angel telling them to leave, he feels they're safe while they're in Egypt. Joseph doesn't want to lose his job at the port especially, when he's making good money.

"We're in Egypt," Joseph says. "His spies won't come here."

5

He dresses up and goes into the city to buy some things. Having earned hundred debens, Egyptian currency at the time, makes him proud of himself. He buys clothes and nappies, which are woollen cloths cut into squares and held in place with pins. Joseph buys provisions and even clothes and flowers for Mary, his wife.

Mary tries to keep baby Jesus out of sight because she's worried someone might recognize him. However, once Joseph presents her with the gifts he'd bought for her, she lets go of her worries and accepts his offer to take her out with baby Jesus. They follow the street towards the sea before they choose a path along the sea and walk for a while.

Joseph is looking here and there at different restaurants. Then, Joseph asks Mary to turn back and return to the inn. The city of Pelusium is still busy as they walk on, and people pass them. He stops in front of a restaurant and speaks.

"This is it. This one will do."

Mary looks up at the sign on the door and sees that it's a Jewish restaurant. A worried look sets on her face.

"Joseph, the baby. They will recognize him in there."

"But we're in Egypt. All that crazy stuff was in Bethlehem and the whole of Judea. Come on let's go in. I promise you if anyone says anything about the baby we're leaving."

Mary thinks it over, standing there on the pavement for a long time. Her push comes when she looks up and down the road laid with cobble stones. Some carriages are passing at that time, a high-ranking Egyptian official's carriage and other carriages stop along the way. Mary with the baby in her arms, rushes towards the restaurant in panic. She fears every authority since Joseph told her of Herod's massacre. She knows the fear is not a holy fear, but it serves to protect her baby. She is afraid that any authority will want to seek her baby's death. Her back is turned, and she stands at the door of the restaurant as the carriage passes.

Joseph doesn't waste time in leading her inside. A line of benches and tables are set in rows in the restaurant. The cashier and attendant stand at a desk placed in the corner against the far wall. Joseph leads Mary and baby Jesus straight across to the desk and demands a table.

"I will like a table for three, please," he says.

"The baby doesn't count," the female attendant says. "You two can choose any table."

She brings out a jar of ink and a feather. Then she asks them.

"What will you two like?"

"The baby counts," Joseph says. "He counts a lot, but I will leave it at that."

The female attendant seems amused by Joseph's comments about the baby. She smiles at him and shakes her head in wonder, then asks him again what they want. Joseph orders their meal before he leads Mary and baby Jesus to a table. When they sit down, Mary moves close to Joseph and asks.

"What were you getting at with the baby counts thing? Don't you realize how important it is to be quiet about this?"

"I just wanted to correct her," Joseph says. "He's going to be the king of the Jews. Why won't he count?"

Mary realizes that Joseph has worked out baby Jesus's coming as Messiah. She says nothing further. Joseph is happy because he's able to provide for his family and they're safe in another land. Although, he still doesn't know how to address the fact that baby Jesus is a holy baby, a child of God. It looks like a mighty task before him.

7

However, he's happy and that is enough for the moment. He pulls Mary closer and plants a kiss on her lips.

"Don't worry about anything, my sweet. God is watching over his child," he says.

"I know," Mary says. "But the heart of the king is wicked."

When their food is served and the attendant walks away, Mary tries to eat and feed baby Jesus from her plate. Since baby Jesus is almost three months old, and she'd breastfeed him before she left, she knows he's not hungry nevertheless, sitting on Mary's lap he's able to pick food from her plate. That happens to be the only place he can sit in the restaurant. They have no facilities for babies or children.

Baby Jesus is trying to pick up food from Mary's plate and put it into his own mouth. In between bites his arms are flapping around, touching this and that. His arms go around Mary like a hug, and he stands up on Mary's lap. Mary holds him with one hand while she uses the other hand to eat.

At the restaurant, people are coming in and out frequently. They're mostly Jews living in Egypt. It so happens that they keep a close community around Pelusium and know every Jew that lives around them. Most of them are looking toward Joseph and Mary with curious gazes. However, nobody approaches them until a woman walks into the restaurant with a walking stick. She attempts to walk past Mary and Joseph.

Baby Jesus is still standing on Mary's lap and chewing on the bit of food he has been able to pick from the plate. He suddenly focuses on the woman as she approaches them. As the woman walks past them, he reaches towards her with his little hand. Smiling, the woman reaches out and touches baby Jesus's hand.

"What a beautiful baby," the woman says.

Just as she touches baby Jesus's finger, she instantly drops her walking stick.

"I'm cured," she shouts.

People around come closer. One person looks at baby Jesus after listening to the woman.

"Lord, where have you been all this time?" He asks.

Mary and Joseph become uncomfortable. Hurriedly they get up without finishing their meal and carry baby Jesus out of the restaurant and don't stop till they get back into their room at the inn. Mary is cross with Joseph for talking her into going to the restaurant. She feels incompetent to deal with baby Jesus even though she knows he's doing a good deed. She feels it's not time for Jesus to get noticed. Without raising her voice, she says.

"I told you it's not a good idea. But you won't listen."

"It's not my fault that your son decides to do a good deed. How am I to know what he will do?" Joseph says. "He's just a baby. How did he know how to do that?"

"I don't know," Mary replies.

"He can't even speak yet," Joseph says. He moves close to baby Jesus where Mary has placed him in his cot. Joseph stares at him.

"What a wonder. God's own child."

Flapping his arms around in the cot, baby Jesus looks directly at him as to say he understands his amazement.

"How do we know how to handle you now?" Joseph asks baby Jesus.

It's clear that Joseph hasn't come to terms with being around baby Jesus. He's frustrated with the situation, as well as feeling lost as a young man having such a burden dumped on him. He's just waking up from being single to being a married young man looking to have a family of his own. However, the twelve weeks they've spent on the road have worn him down and he can't think of getting on the road again so soon.

So, Joseph doesn't think of running away. He agrees with Mary that it's best if she and baby Jesus stay indoors from now on. Another reason Joseph is not looking at running away is that he wants to work and earn more money. As it stands, they have nothing to live on. On their twelve weeks journey from Bethlehem, they've spent the gold that the three wise men gave to baby Jesus. The frankincense he'd exchanged for a room. They've only got the myrrh left, and he can't think of how to turn it into money.

For now, Joseph is working on a boat at the docks. He wants to finish the job, because he will be paid more on completing the job. So, he goes to work for the next two weeks while Mary and baby Jesus spend most of their time in the room. On Joseph's last day on the boat, he's clearing out his tools when he overhears people talking.

"They said the holy baby escaped to Egypt, and someone said he has spotted him here," says a man.

"I haven't heard that," replies one of the boat crew.

Joseph moves closer. The person speaking is a Jew asking people if they've seen the holy baby. He's an old man dressed as an Egyptian, wearing a long white gown with a head band that he wraps around his face. Joseph looks at the man, who looks back at Joseph. He tries to move toward Joseph.

Joseph picks up his tool-box, and walks out, leaving the man staring at him. He quickly finds the captain and collects his money. On reaching the inn, he finds Gosham the innkeeper talking with some men.

"These men don't believe me that there's a holy baby in this inn. I know because I've seen him myself." Gosham says.

10

When he sees Joseph coming, he stops talking until Joseph walks past. As soon as he walks past, Joseph hears Gosham's soft whisper.

"That's the man with the baby. I had to let them stay for free."

Joseph runs to his room and shuts the door behind him. Mary is sleeping, with baby Jesus beside her on the bed. Joseph wakes Mary and tells her what he overheard. He even tells her about Gosham, blabbing away about a holy baby in his inn.

"We're not safe here anymore," Mary says, instantly in panic. "They can be anybody. I mean, anybody can be Herod's spy."

"Let's leave tonight," Joseph says. "I've made some money that will keep us going for a while."

Joseph realizes he was wrong to assume Herod's spies won't come into Egypt. Without another thought, both gather their things and get baby Jesus ready. Within a few minutes they're ready to go.

They leave through the back door without letting the inn-keeper know, and they travel out of the city towards an unknown destination. They leave Pelusium and go south towards the next city to find refuge for their baby. This is their aim: to keep baby Jesus away from Herod's spies because they know that anyone asking about a holy baby could only be Herod's spy. Being a stranger in Egypt doesn't help much, because Joseph needs to rely on passing Jews in Egypt or a good Egyptian, and there are only a few of them.

The worry stays with him as they travel with baby Jesus. He thinks of what baby Jesus will call him when he starts to talk. He thinks about how baby Jesus is to become the king of the Jews and save them from their sins. Joseph worries about baby Jesus's upbringing.

He also wants to know how to control baby Jesus's good

deeds so that it does not give them away. Somehow, he knows there will be more good deeds to come but where and when he doesn't know. Joseph knows this because he believes in the prophets, what they've spoken about Jesus. Joseph believes Jesus is the Messiah and appreciates the honour that is bestowed on him to be an earthly father to baby Jesus.

Chapter 2

LEARNING TO CRAWL

After leaving Pelusium in the night, the family journeys southward and of course Joseph is leading the way. Mary is still worried about how they've left Gosham without a word. She thinks at least they could've said thank you to him and let him know they we're leaving. But Joseph is having none of it.

"Gosham is a man after his own heart. He's doing nothing but making money out of every situation. Otherwise, why is he telling people he let us stay for free? What about the frankincense I gave him?"

He leads them out of the city boundary, and they walk through the night into the countryside, walking on dusty roads with wild forest on both sides. In the sky there are thousands of stars shining brightly. The stars don't tell the suffering this holy baby is bearing. The family left their donkey back in Pelusium in a hurry and must make do with their feet. Mary has baby Jesus in her arms and carries a single bag that contains their possessions.

As he leads them along, Joseph is thinking. He wonders how exactly Herod knew he hadn't killed the holy child in his massacre. *"How did he know we're in Egypt? This isn't a way for a king to live and use his authority."* He thinks to himself and looks back over his shoulder at Mary and the child.

They've walked out of the city of Pelusium completely and he can still see that they're nowhere near another city. It's getting dark. He doesn't want to push Mary into the deep of the night with a newborn in her arms. So, as they walk on, he's on the look-out for some place they can spend the night. He walks and looks for what seems like an hour before he notices in the distance a mountain in the forest near to the road.

He stops and looks at Mary.

"Mary it will be nice if we stop for the night so that the baby can sleep."

"Where do we find a place in this wilderness?" Mary asks.

"God willing, we'll find a place on that mountain," Joseph points to the mountain and says.

They leave the road and branch onto the rough path leading to the mountain. It's dark but the moon above them gives them light. They arrive at the mountain and find a cave just at the base. Joseph makes a fire with wood and grass he gathers. Afterward he gathers leaves, wood, and grass to make a bed for baby Jesus. Mary lays him down on the bed a distance away from the fire while Joseph gets their own bed ready.

The look on Mary's face shows that she's tired, but who wouldn't be. Not long after giving birth she had to make a tremendous journey into another land. And once they're there, they can't stay in one place. The journey from Bethlehem could have been shorter if they didn't have to stop for the night every now and then. At times they set off late in the morning and still must find a way to feed the newborn.

Mary looks weary, but a nice night's sleep will make up for it. By the time Joseph finishes making their sleeping place, baby Jesus is sound asleep with the glow from the fire dancing on him lightly. Mary and Joseph cuddle up together and fall asleep but not before Joseph says.

"Mary, you know this baby is the child of God. Do you think he will know me as his father? Who will he call father?"

Mary turns to her husband and smiles, looking right into his eyes.

"My dear husband," she says. "There will be lots of time for you to prove to him that you're his stepfather."

"So, I'm not his father."

"How can you be? He's the child of God."

"But isn't all Israel," Joseph says. "Israel is God's child."

"Joseph, you talk like you don't believe anymore," Mary says with concern in her voice.

"No, no, Mary," Joseph says.

Realizing the disappointment in Mary's voice, Joseph knows that if he says he doesn't believe God's word, it will be a sin. But Joseph is worried and concerned more for Mary and the baby's health. It bothers him that they must keep running in a strange land just to get out of death's reach.

"I believe he's God's child because I know I didn't do it, and the angel appeared to me as well. I can't deny it. God is really with us. See how far we've come and we're still alive."

"He will never leave his son alone," Mary says and turns on her side. Soon she falls asleep.

Joseph lies awake still turning things around in his mind. He's reflecting on the miracle God performed to bring baby Jesus to life. He thinks of how he could have planted the baby in Mary's womb, and he's left speechless and baffled.

Of course, Joseph is baffled just like any man would be. How difficult it must be to see your woman pregnant with a baby that isn't yours and to know the formidable bafflement that it belongs to God. He doesn't know whether to envy or respect God. He knows his first reaction to divorce her secretly was out of respect for God's commandment, which has become their own law. It's a law and the purpose of the secrecy is not to bring harm to her.

That was before the angel of God appeared to him and told him not to think of it anymore. "Do not be afraid to take Mary as your wife, because the pregnancy in her is a holy child."

He ponders everything over and over before he finally sleeps. The morning comes with a sweet smell of the forest blowing in through the small opening into the cave. Baby Jesus lies awake on his hay bed and stares into the dying campfire. The campfire that had burned out suddenly rekindles and burns, bringing warmth into the cave. He smiles and lies there looking at the fire.

Mary and Joseph wake up later and Joseph sits there looking at the fire, then he turns to Mary.

"How's that fire still burning?"

Mary looks at the fire. There's no wood left in the fire, only coals and ash, but the flame is burning high.

"The lord is looking after us. He knows we need the warmth," Mary says. She then spots baby Jesus smiling at the fire. "Look at him smiling. He likes it."

"Maybe he did it," Joseph says, rising.

"He doesn't know what fire is yet," Mary says. "He's got a name, you know."

Joseph walks out of the cave without another word. He finds a surprise waiting for him. Animals are grazing in the field in front of the cave. The animals are small with long ears like hares. Instead of running they stay, even when Joseph walks into the woods and finds a good long stick that can knock them dead. He walks close to them, and they look up at him, then back down

16

again. Joseph just picks one up, puts it under his arm while it is still alive and walks into the cave with it.

"See what I've got," he says. "Mary, breakfast, lunch and dinner. They're all out there grazing in the field. He must have done something."

"Who's he?" Mary says. "I told you he's got a name. A beautiful name chosen by God himself. The angel told me."

"What's his name then? Because you haven't told me since. All I know is what I see."

"Haven't you seen enough to believe?"

"I believe," Joseph says, still dangling the little animal from his hand. "Who tells you that I don't believe," he asks fearing it might be an angel.

"The way you sounded last night doesn't sound like you believe," Mary says. "You even avoid calling him by his name."

"What do you want me to do now, woman?"

"Call him by his name. His name is Jesus. The angel says it."

"I know the angel says it, Mary."

"Then why are you not calling him that?"

"I'm just getting there, woman. Give me a chance. You know everything has been hectic since you got pregnant. Now see where we are. Just let me make breakfast so we eat before we start going again." He starts to turn around but stops and speaks. "Don't you think we should give him another name we can call him?"

"Why, Joseph?" Mary says.

"I just thought a pet name might be good to call him by because his God given name is a name of power. Think about it while I get breakfast ready, and we can go."

"Go where? I'm not going anywhere yet."

17

Joseph says nothing but holds the animal and tries to break its' neck. Mary stops him.

"Stop," she says. "If you kill that animal now, where are you going to get the water to wash it."

"Now that you say it, I don't know."

He looks around him and sees no water. Mary says.

"Why don't you go outside and look around? Maybe there's a river nearby."

Joseph drops the animal in the cave and walks outside the cave. Mary follows him outside with baby Jesus in her arms, and they stand outside the cave entrance and look at the animals grazing in the field.

"If I can have my way," Mary says, "I will have a spring here along the field here. So, the grazing animals could drink and that will be useful to us as well."

"Too bad, your son doesn't know what a spring is," Joseph says.

"I didn't mean Jesus. I was only saying."

"But we need water. Isn't that what you said?"

Joseph walks further heading towards the forest nearby. Mary, on the other hand places baby Jesus on the ground and he plays with the animals, pulling their small tails and fur. They didn't run away. They allow him to hold them while they hop around him. Then, baby Jesus touches the ground and scoops dust into his hand. He's coming close to four months now and his grip is strong.

Mary turns quickly to see him scoop the dust, and she walks towards him to clean off his hand. When she gets closer, she sees the spot from where baby Jesus scooped up dust and finds water springing from the ground. He dips his baby hand into the water and splashes it. Mary rushes away quickly, calling Joseph.

"Joseph, I've found water. Come quickly."

Joseph runs out of the forest. Mary leads him back to baby Jesus and shows him the spring of water. Joseph is speechless. He stares at the water and then at baby Jesus for a long time knowing that he did it.

"Thanks be to God," he says at last. "Let's have something to eat, then we can wash ourselves as well."

Joseph takes another animal and goes inside the cave. Mary washes baby Jesus in the spring of water, washing his hair and body before she wraps him up and carries him inside. Joseph has two of the animals roasting on the campfire.

"Food will be ready soon." he says. 'Will the baby eat some as well?"

"Joseph," Mary says. "He's only four months old. I will breast feed him."

"Then you will have to eat a lot for the two of you."

"You should have said that when I was pregnant with him."

Joseph stops turning the roast and looks over to Mary where she sits on a small rock, dressing baby Jesus. When she was pregnant, he wasn't sure whether to stay or run. Now, he's just contented with his wife and his family. He wants to do everything possible to prove he's a worthy man. Where God himself is involved, he can't argue against it. He's still not sure what God has in plan for him and Mary, but whatever it is he knows it will be good.

"Are you cross with me because I didn't say that then?" he asks.

"No, love. It would've suited the occasion then because that's when you eat for two."

"Oh, oh, I see." He bends down and turns the roast over. "I will go find something to go along with this meat. I should find something in the forest there."

Joseph rises and walks towards the exit. Mary is already breast-feeding baby Jesus but she looks up.

"Don't be long, sweetie."

Joseph walks out of the cave and stops. He can't believe what he's seeing in front of him. On the field near to the spring, on the spot where Mary washed baby Jesus balsam flowers have grown in purple, pink, red, blue and yellow colours all together. They are so beautiful in their colourful array. Joseph wipes his eyes in disbelief. Then he calls out.

"Mary, come quickly. Come and see this."

"I'm feeding the baby," Mary shouts. "Can't it wait?"

Joseph says nothing but plucks some flowers and shoots. He walks into the forest and finds potatoes and berries that he picks and brings back. Mary is at the cave entrance with baby Jesus in her arms. She is gazing at the balsam flowers with beautiful surprise written all over her face. She looks at the baby in her arms.

"You did this, didn't you?" She walks up and meets Joseph. "This's the spot I washed him," she says. "See how flowers grow on the spot."

"That's what I was calling you to come and see."

"I know, isn't it beautiful?" Mary says "Blessed be the name of the Lord."

They walk back inside the cave and Joseph prepares the meal, roasting the potatoes and the meat and spices he picked from the forest, along with balsam flowers. They eat and afterwards Mary lays baby Jesus down and falls asleep herself. Joseph is out and about gathering woods from the forest and building things. He builds a table and chairs and even a cot for baby Jesus to sleep in.

By the time Mary wakes up eight hours later, Joseph had finished making a bed for them as well. All the while, baby Jesus lies in his hay bed and gazes everywhere. He smiles a lot and sometimes just gazes curiously. He doesn't make any noise or yell and the only time he cries is when Mary wakes up, and it's late afternoon.

She walks over to him and picks him up before she walks out of the cave. She walks into the fading sunshine and stops, looking at Joseph and all the stuff he'd made. She sees the baby cot and her heart melts. She walks over to him and gives him a hug and a kiss.

"Thank you," she says.

"I thought if we're going to stay here longer, we might as well have a bed to sleep in."

"That's very thoughtful of you, my dear."

Joseph has made two sitting chairs and a table, so, he places one chair near the cave entrance and asks her to sit down. Mary sits and holds baby Jesus in her arms. Joseph moves everything inside the cave and sets it all up before he calls Mary to come and see. They spend three more days in the cave.

On their last day after the morning meal, Mary takes baby Jesus outside to the field and sets him down among the balsam flowers. She plays with him, calling him to her, and watches him trying to reach for her. Joseph is busy making more items to while away his time. Baby Jesus makes his first attempt to reach Mary a few yards from him. He gets on his hands and knees and crawls on the grass over to his mother. Mary is overjoyed. She scoops him up in her arms and shouts.

"Hallelujah! Glory be to God! My son is crawling."

Joseph stops what he's doing.

"Joseph, he's crawling at just four months."

"I wonder what he will do next." Joseph says and continues with what he's doing.

The following morning, they set off away from the cave after spending four days there. They get back on the road and continue to travel southward. They are about to enter the town of Tel- Basta when they meet with some travellers, trades men and trades women travelling in a carriage. The traders offer to give the family a ride, and on their way, they discuss Herod. One of them introduces himself.

"My name is Joel. I've been travelling this road for years with goods all the way from Judea. I'm going to Tahpanhes, where I have a shop. You see, all these Jews running over into Egypt lately is good for Egypt but bad for Judea and Herod. He's a ruling ape now. Every citizen of Judea hates him. He knows that, so he makes life even more difficult for them. He has raised taxes twice and requires every new baby to be registered before their first birthday. I hope you're not thinking of going back just yet."

"No, no, not at all." says Joseph.

"I hope your baby wasn't born in Judea." says another man, making Joseph realize they know where they're from.

"We've been in Egypt for a while now and barely know what's going on in Judea," Joseph says. "Tell me more, Joel. What is King Herod like, these days?"

"Oh, my goodness. The man has become a monster. He killed all these babies for nothing. Recently, I heard he sent his spies into Judea and its' neighbours asking for a holy child."

"Maybe it's the holy child he wants," says a woman.

"I won't have my baby and give him to Herod to kill," says the other woman. "God forbid. I will run as far as I can get with my baby."

Mary knows from what the woman said that she's doing what any mother will do for her son, even though it was God himself who set them on the journey. They reach Tel- Basta and Mary and Joseph stop there. The group continues with the journey but for Joseph that's the end of the road. During the discussion on the wagon, Joel told them that Herod has spies even in Egypt. This confirms Joseph's suspicions.

"Lots of them are walking around Tahpanhes," Joel says. "Herod is still in panic that a holy child is going to rule over Israel and take his throne away. Everyone knows it and they all just laugh at him."

Having heard that, Joseph makes up his mind to take his family down south. He believes there're no spies lurking around in the south as they're all up north and close to the border. Joseph is concerned about the many miles they must travel with a new baby. So, as they go along, he makes sure they have good rest. Babies get weary of journeys quickly, and having no means of transport is a barrier. They find a small cave in Tel Basta to stay for two days before they continue southward toward the city of Belbeis.

⁓ Chapter 3 ⁓

LEARNING TO TALK

As the family progresses from Tel Basta they travel further south. Joseph hopes that if they stay away from Jews like themselves, there will be little to no problem. With this thought in mind, he leads the family towards Belbeis, stopping only for the night in caves. Mary straps baby Jesus onto herself with a cloth to make the walk easier. And, while they walk, she sings and tells him stories to keep him busy on the road until he goes to sleep. When they eventually stop for the night in a cave, Joseph is quick in getting a fire going and a place to sleep for the baby first before he makes their own.

They often stay up together long after baby Jesus has gone to bed. The necessary thing in the morning is feeding baby Jesus and washing him. Somehow, they've been able to find sustenance for themselves through the journey.

It's like God has set signs and wonders to follow them everywhere they go. Food and water come easily, and the only thing they need to worry about is people finding out who they are. They know that will be dangerous for baby Jesus. They don't mind the wonders if they're kept undercover and so often, they're alone in a cave or on a mountain side.

They reach Belbeis three days after leaving Tel Basta and try to find sustenance among the Egyptians there. Belbeis is a small city set within the branches of the Nile. It has a river running through it. At the edge of the city is another river and both rivers run into the Nile. The houses there are built close together with some facing each other while others have their back to the road. Other houses are scattered.

Along the river lies lots of parchment drying out with kids watching over them. From the size of the city Joseph knows there will be a small number of Jews around there. But, they don't find anything to eat until late evening, when an Egyptian hears the cry of baby Jesus and asks them to come in. Mary sits on a small wall in front of a house and tries to feed baby Jesus, but he continues to cry.

"You can't feed the baby out here," says the Egyptian tradesman who sees them outside his shop. "Come inside here, please." He leads them through his shop into a living area at the back.

"We've been trying to find a place to stay." Joseph says to the man. "How hard can it be to find a room for the night?"

"Unless you carry big money, you won't find a room. The Romans are coming. Everyone is talking about it that the pharaoh is not strong anymore to hold them back."

"Is that why they don't welcome strangers," Mary asks. She has noticed how withdrawn the people are. They seem not to care about them. Mary has a cloth draped over her chest and feeds baby Jesus while she talks. She looks worried and distressed.

"They fear the war coming," says the shop owner.

"I thought something was wrong," Mary says.

She reflects again on how they've been turned down from every inn and house they've approached since they arrived in Belbeis early afternoon. Some innkeepers said that babies are not allowed, and some said they have no rooms for family. Others charged high price that they can't afford. Finally, they got weary and sat on the wall in front of his shop.

They realize they're near the edge of the city, on the outskirts. The few houses that are left before the city limit are remote, and few people wander into them if they're not living around here. As soon as they step inside, the shop owner must attend to customers in the shop. He stayed in the shop for hours, and they're left alone in the living room.

Mary feeds baby Jesus and lays him down on a small bed they put together. Then the two of them sit and wait for the shop owner to return. Baby Jesus is sound asleep when the shop owner comes back inside, and by that time it's dark and late.

"Whoa, I've never seen so many people flow through here before," says the shop owner while finding a place to sit.

"Why is it different today?" asks Joseph who is suspicious. "Did they say what they're looking for around here?"

"Nope. They said they're wandering around. Why? Is there anything going on around here that I should know about?"

"No, no, not at all," Joseph says. "I was just curious like you, about why people are coming around here."

"Gee, it beats me what they want. Whatever they want, I say you people bring good luck to my house."

The man makes food, and they eat. While they're eating Joseph speaks.

"Have you got a spare room where we can stay for a few days? I will work for you to pay for our stay if you want that."

The man doesn't think twice but leans over the table and offers his hand.

"My name is Malek. You and your family bring good luck to my house. You can stay as long as you want. You can start work in the morning. I will need help in the shop."

Malek shows them their room. They move baby Jesus in there and go to sleep themselves. As it turns out Malek doesn't have a child anymore. He explains to them that his son and his wife died of a disease.

"Egypt has too many plagues," Malek says.

In the morning Joseph starts at the shop with Malek. He builds an extension and arranges tables and chairs for people to sit and have their drinks. They stay with Malek at the shop in Belbeis for four weeks. However, Joseph fears the worst as the days go on and the day baby Jesus says his first word comes within his fears.

Mary, as always, stays in the house tending to baby Jesus and the house. She dreams of a time she will be able to tend her own house and family. Softly she prays in her heart. "God, please bring this over in time. Let this be over." After she cleans the house, she bathes baby Jesus and sings to him as she does.

One day in their fourth week in Belbeis, she is bathing him and singing a song while he sits in the bath. Although, the angel of God tells them to name him Jesus, they still want to give him a second name, like Joseph suggested, an ordinary name that does not connote power. The name they choose is Isa. So, Mary often calls him Isa, like on this very morning.

"Isa, say mama," she says. "You should be speaking by now."

Baby Jesus looks at her and shakes his head.

"What does that mean, Isa? Say mama," she repeats. "I carried you for nine months. I'm your mother."

Joseph walks in on them and sees her getting frustrated over baby Jesus not saying the word, *mama*.

"Give him a chance, Mary," Joseph says. "He's only how old now, four months? He still has a long way to go before he starts to speak."

"He's five months and hasn't said a word," Mary says.

"Then ask God. Don't frustrate the child."

As the two of them speak, a little voice says.

"Mama."

Mary and Joseph stop talking and stare at the baby. He smiles and says it again.

"Mama." Then he claps his little hands together.

Mary is so happy that she jumps up and dances.

"I'm his mama," she sings. Joseph watches her. Then she stops and points to Joseph.

"Say papa," she says.

Baby Jesus looks at her and shakes his head. Then he does an amazing thing. He points upward to the sky and speaks.

"Papa."

"That boy knows who he is," Joseph says and adds. "He won't call me father. Will he now?"

He walks out feeling disappointed. Mary doesn't know what to say. She merely stares at her baby in surprise. Then at long last she says.

"God knows who you are."

She lifts him out of the water and throws away the bath water. In the courtyard where Mary throws the bath water, on the edges of the pool where the water runs, balsam flowers have sprouted. Mary is in wonder, but Joseph is in a vigilant mood. He keeps wondering where all these people are coming from and what they want around there.

Malek is happy the business is growing. Joseph can't stay quiet anymore. So, as he delivers drinks to a family of six, he asks.

"Where are you people going? What are you looking for around here?"

"I feel that God is around here," says the woman in the family.

She's large, you could've taken her for a giant. The man is almost about her size but a bit shorter. He comes out straight.

"God is here and we're moving here."

"Oh, ooh, I see," Joseph says. He sees how they look at him awkwardly. "What makes you so sure of that?" He asks.

"I see his star," the man says.

Joseph gazes across the land where he can see different types of tents pitched around them with families living in them. Now he understands what's going on. He knows it's baby Jesus they're there for. There's no doubt in his mind, so after serving them he finds a chance to go inside to Mary. She's dressed and has fed baby Jesus and is trying to get him to sleep when Joseph walks in.

"What are we going to do now?" he says, looking distressed.

He feels downhearted thinking they must move again. He just wants a home he can call his own and to settle down with his family. Having to be on the move so much is draining him of necessary energy. Mary notices his downcast mood and comes to him.

"What's the problem now?" She asks.

"It's these people. They are coming here to live because your baby is here."

"How do you know that?" asks Mary in a hushed tone.

"I asked them," Joseph says. "They said they come here because God is here. I think you haven't been outside in a while. I say you go outside and see what's going on."

It's true. For the four weeks they've been there Mary and baby Jesus haven't stepped outside the courtyard of the house. The house has a wide courtyard behind it, where they sit after Mary has done the cleaning. She lays a mat on the floor, places baby Jesus on it, and plays with him until the sun goes down or he goes to sleep.

29

Mary does go outside after baby Jesus goes to sleep. She lays him down in their room and walks outside to the road. She can't believe her eyes at the throng of people flowing through the area. She walks around to see the many tents pitched up around them. Then she realizes Joseph's fear and panic herself.

As it turns out it's not only the Jews who are awaiting signs. Even the Egyptians can read it in the sky. Prophets who foretold the coming of God's son proclaimed that signs and wonders would follow him. It's little wonder why so many people gather around him. And Mary fears this so much at this time of their despair.

"We can't stay here anymore," she says to Joseph, back in the house.

"I know," Joseph says. "But I think as long as Herod's spies don't come among them, we might be safe."

"How do you know who's a spy among all these people?" Mary asks.

"The person asking questions around will be a spy. Just listen when you're among them."

"I'm not bringing my baby out there to meet all these people," Mary says feeling jealous over her baby. "They will rip him apart."

"We won't stay here any longer once I notice a spy among them.' Joseph says and assures her.

Mary believes him because she knows Joseph cares about the welfare of herself and the baby. She knows the fear of God is in him and he won't allow any harm to come to the child even though he knows he's not his child. For a whole week afterward nothing happens, and they continue to live with Malek the shop owner until a barmy day at the end of the week.

The sun is out, and people are drinking and playing. Joseph is serving drinks to people when a well- dressed man stops him.

The man holds on to his arm so that Joseph must grip the tray in his hand.

"Please, can you tell me where I can find the holy child?" the man says.

Joseph stares at the man unbelievably until it occurs to him that he's staring and not talking.

"Look over there in the tents," he says.

"Oh yes, of course," says the man. "It has to be the tent." He walks away.

Joseph at once turns back and runs inside. He tells Mary what happened and that he thinks, the man is a spy for Herod.

"Trust nobody that asks questions," he says.

Mary agrees with him and together they pack their bags. They leave in the night, with baby Jesus strapped to Mary. Malek tries to stop them. He offers to pay Joseph for working with him and even offers them money and asks them to stay. Joseph takes the money knowing they will need it on their way.

"We must go Malek. The baby's health is at risk."

Malek seems to object looking at the baby strapped to Mary's chest. He seems to want to say the baby is fine, and Joseph is hoping he won't say that. Finally, looking over at Joseph and seeing he's not joking. Malek spreads his arms and speaks.

"I guess you must go if you must go. May God be with you."

"Thank you, Malek. You've been of immense help," Joseph says. "May the mercies of God be with you." They hug and part ways.

They leave and set off southward again. Mary's heart aches for the comfort of Malek's house but thinking of the danger around, she forgets and adjusts to the road. She has one thing to say about Malek as they go.

"He's a God-fearing man. He talks about God and not the Egyptian gods."

"I wonder which god he means," Joseph says. "He's had his reward from the people your son brought to his shop. And I worked for him. So, he can't complain."

Mary did want to ask Joseph how he knows it's baby Jesus that made the people come but she doesn't, having heard Joseph's mind on the matter. She does wonder, though, if it's really her son that all these people are looking for and keeps quiet on the matter. The family continues southwards with Joseph explaining to Mary that the farther south they travel, the farther they will be from a Jewish community, and then they can find refuge among the Egyptians.

∽ *Chapter 4* ∾

HEROD'S GRIEF

In his massively large bedroom with a massive bed in the
middle, King Herod is sleeping beside his second wife, Herodine. Suddenly, towards the early hour of the morning, King
Herod jumps up from his sleep.

"Oh my goodness! Why won't he die?" He shouts. "It's him
again. He runs away. Where did he run to? I must find him."

His wife wakes up.

"What's the problem, Herod?" she asks.

"It's that child. He won't die. I've looked all over Judea and
Galilee. They can't find him."

"Which child?"

"The child they said will rule the Jews. I keep seeing him in
my dreams."

"But I thought you've killed them all."

"I can still see him. I can't close my eyes without seeing him.
He's in my dreams. In my head. He must die. He just has to die.
Nobody takes my throne while I'm alive. And I know the man
for the job."

He walks into his closet and while he's in there his wife can
still hear him telling himself that the child must die. She thinks
he's going crazy, because after the large massacre he ordered in

Judea, he has never been the same again, fretting nonstop about a child taking his throne. How Israel would become one under the child and he would rule them all. She thinks a newborn couldn't come to rule the Jews tomorrow. It's far-fetched. It must be her son who rules next.

Hearing his wife's confidence is not enough for Herod. He just seems to lack confidence where this child is concerned. Ten minutes later Herod comes out all dressed up in a brown tunic with designs in gold and matching trousers. Over this, he puts on a large over coat with golden designs on it as well. Then he sits his crown on his head.

"How did I look, darling?" he asks.

"You look like always, gorgeous."

"Thank you, my dear. But I don't feel that way right now," he says, then adds quickly. "Now, about this child. I must see Namhiba. He knows how to recruit people for spies."

He walks into his throne hall and sits on his throne, tapping his feet on the floor. Soon a guard walks in from outside and presents himself before King Herod.

"Call Namhiba," Herod says.

The guard walks out, and Herod is by himself again until his chiefs and law makers walk in. They talk to him about the new law he proposed which is to pay tax according to the land you own.

Throughout the conversation Herod's mind is on the holy child. It's like he keeps seeing him everywhere he looks. The same awkward image of a baby sitting on his throne flashes into his mind. He looks at his chiefs and lawmakers.

"I want a new law to go along with the last one."

"What new law is that, Your Highness?" asks one of the chiefs.

"I want all new residents into Judea to be registered, along with their family roots in Judea. Everyone newly arrived, be it alien or Jews, must register their name upon entering this land. I want to know everyone in my kingdom."

"That will be a nice gesture. Your Highness," says a lawmaker.

"That's what I thought as well," Herod replies.

Namhiba arrives with the same guard, and King Herod postpones every other conversation to speak to him. Like Herod, he's not a tall man. Instead, he's short and large with a massive head that says he has lots to think about. Be it reality or folklores, big heads are often counted as big ideas. But that stands to be seen as Herod speaks with Namhiba.

"I have a problem, Namhiba," he says. "You see there's still a child who got away from the killing I commanded in Judea."

"A child? How sir?" asks Namhiba.

"I don't know. All I know is that he got away, and they travelled somewhere else. Where I don't know."

"What must we do, Your Highness?" Namhiba asks.

"I want you to hire spies and send them into all Judea, Galilee, Samaria, Lebanon, and Egypt. As far and as close as possible. I want them to find this holy child for me."

"But, Your Highness must realize that we can't kill him there even if we find him."

"You can steal the baby from his mother and bring him to me. Can't you?"

"Yes, Your Highness. We can do that much."

"So go and do that." Herod says. "I want this child found. God can't play me now that I know he's still alive. I will find him and end this threat to my throne."

It's true Herod feels threatened by baby Jesus's birth. He feels his throne is at risk and his bloodline would never be the Jewish royalty again. His days and nights are consumed by what he terms as his nightmare. He's ready to defend his throne and bloodline no matter who comes in his way. Hearing that a child has been born that will eventually become the king of the Jews throws him away into something else.

He knows it's God who is working in the child because the wise men say, he's a holy child. Not knowing how to fight God, he embarks on his killing spree. Since that wasn't enough, he's still not satisfied.

Namhiba leaves him to carry out his command and Herod returns to his law makers. He knows that the law he's making now will seal every way possible for any child to come back into Judea and rule them. He smiles to himself, feeling at ease for the first time this morning.

Later as the chiefs and lawmakers are making their way out. Herodine, his wife, comes in wearing a large purple gown that spreads behind her. She walks to the throne, and when Herod sees her, his sins visit him again. He remembers how he'd taken her from his rivals. He'd had them killed before he married her. He knows it's for the glory. Not that he cares for a soul but only for his own glory. He believes he's a god in his own right. Herodine sits next to him and says,

"What have you done now, Herod?"

"Nothing," he says.

"What about that child you're going on about? Have you done anything about it?"

"Yeah, about that. I've sent Namhiba out for spies to kidnap the child and bring him to me."

"So, you're kidnapping one of your own subjects, instead of commanding them."

"What will you have me do now?" Herod asks. "The child has gone into another territory. He's in the kingdom of the Samaritans or Egyptians by now. I can't command him from there."

All the chiefs and lawmakers have gone now except for Herod and Herodine. Both sit and talk, then suddenly a woman walks down from the entrance. Herod watches her as she approaches. The woman stops in front of the throne and speaks.

"I can't even bow to you, Herod. No, not anymore. You and your wife are murderers. Even all your chiefs. You're all murderers. You killed my son. You killed my son, my baby. God will punish you for this Herod. You shall be punished for every child's soul you took away."

Herod is frightened looking at the woman. His fright is not about the woman or what she's saying. It's the fact that she managed to reach his presence without being stopped. He cries out.

"Russel! Russel!" He calls while the woman keeps talking. Nobody shows up, not even a guard. "Gordon, Gordon!" he calls again.

"Herod, you won't live your days in full," the woman says. "You shall die like everyone else." She turns to Herodine and speaks. "You, Herodine, you're not a woman but a beast, because you allowed him to do what he did. Killing all these children. The two of you together are beasts. You're monsters," the woman yells. "Monsters! Monsters is what you are."

One of the guards must have heard her yells and comes inside. Then, he calls out to more guards and four guards rush inside and approach her.

"Where has everybody gone? You lots are in trouble," Herod says as the guards pull the woman out. "You lots are not on your duty. I will have all of you skinned out."

The guards manage to drag the woman out of the throne hall. Herod turns his attention to his wife and speaks.

"Can you believe this? They allowed that woman to enter my

presence. Suppose she came to kill us. She would have done the job, and nobody would have seen her."

"I'm shocked as well. What's this palace turning into? Herod you need to take proper control of this situation. Your officers are relinquishing their duties."

"I know, my dear. Is it my fault? I feed and keep them, yet they can't protect me."

Herod sits and ponders on things. It's not every day you're visited by your sins. That's only for the conscientious, but Herod isn't conscientious. In fact, he's far from it. He's not thinking about what he has done or everything the woman said. They didn't bother him as much as the fact that his guards let her into his presence.

Herod is furious with his palace officials. And, he's still pondering on that with his wife sitting beside him when he suddenly looks up. In the middle of the room, standing in the middle of the air, is a baby who couldn't be more than two years old, with a golden crown on his head. Bright lights surround him, and his garment is sparkling with light. Herod wipes his eyes to see properly, thinking he's dreaming. He nudges his wife.

"Can you see him?" he asks, pointing at the image.

"I can't see anything." says Herodine. "What exactly can you see?"

Herod doesn't reply to her question. He gazes frozen at the image before him, then he says.

"Are you the one they say will be king of the Jews?"

No response comes to him, and he gets agitated and speaks.

"I am the king of the Jews. I am Herod the great, king of the Jews. Not you and it shall not be. I will find you and put an end to this charade."

He gets up and moves towards the middle of the room as he

talks. But a few steps away from the image he stops. The infant in the image points a finger at him. Suddenly Herod's ears open, and he hears babies, lots of them crying in his head. He falls to his kneel before the image grabbing hold of his ears. He holds his two ears, rising again and walking back to his seat frustrated.

"Can you hear that?" He asks, leaning into his wife.

"I can't hear anything, and I can't see anything you're talking to," she says. "You're not yourself anymore. You're acting like a crazy man. Oh, how it would sound if Judea should hear that their king is going crazy over a little child."

"Seriously," Herod says. "I can hear babies crying. Lots of them."

"There are no babies here I can see. Come let's go inside. You might be thinking too much." She rises and holds his hand.

"But I'm expecting some delegates from Galilee this afternoon."

"You're in no position to hold a meeting. Look at you. You're crazy over a little child."

Herod stands up and she holds his hand as they both walk away from the throne room. He continues to hear the cries of the babies even when the image disappears.

Chapter 5

FIRST TOOTH

A day away into their journey southward, baby Jesus takes ill. His face is drawn in and he has no smile left in him. They've left the harsh temperature of the desert behind and are moving towards the Nile. They rest for the night in a small cave and in the morning when Mary wants to pick him up to prepare him for the journey ahead, she's instantly worried and in panic.

"Joseph," she calls. "Something is wrong with Isa." She lifts him up and sees how hot he feels. "He's running a temperature."

Joseph arrives by her side. He knows something is wrong at once when he sees baby Jesus. His bright eyes are dim. His colour fading, turning pale. Joseph watches him more closely and seems confused at what could be the problem with God's own child.

"Try and feed him," he says. "See if he will eat."

Mary tries but baby Jesus isn't responding and then she notices that his cheeks are red. She opens his mouth and feels his gums. She can tell they're swollen and red.

"Joseph, I think he's having his first tooth," she says. "Look, his cheeks are red. And his gums are swollen."

"That's why he won't eat then," Joseph says.

"Oh, my poor baby," Mary moans. "Now he's not going to be able to eat."

"Give him a cold wash and let's get going," Joseph says.

He gets their things ready to get moving from the cave again. He knows they have less than a day to travel before they reach the next town. His intention to take the family down south appears to be a bright one so far. Mary hasn't argued with him because she trusts him. She knows he worries about the welfare of herself and the baby. She carries baby Jesus to a pond that swells from the ground around them.

The pond is cold and soothing as she pours the cold water on baby Jesus. His temperature seems to go down, but it doesn't last, because as soon as they're moving again, baby Jesus starts getting hot again. Mary can feel him against her body, because he's strapped to her chest. She feels how hot he gets and how restless his sleep is.

"Joseph, my baby is getting hotter again by the minute," she says.

"We're near to a town," he replies. "We'll stop there for a few days for him to grow his teeth."

They enter the town of Mostorod near to evening. Most of the towns people are out in their front courtyard with children playing. The first house they see, Mary in her haste goes there and asks for help.

"Please, somebody help me. My son is sick," she says.

A woman comes out of the house and calls her inside.

"Don't worry," she says. "I'm a mother as well. We'll do our best to make your son well. What's the problem with him?"

"I think it's his first tooth. He's running so much temperature, and I don't know how to cool him down."

Instantly the woman goes outside into her courtyard and prepares a bath in a large bathing bowl. After she prepares the bath, she calls to Mary.

"Give him a bath in there. It's a cold bath with soothing oil and herbs. It will calm his feverish temperature down."

"Thank you," Mary says.

She prepares baby Jesus for a bath. Then she looks to the woman and asks.

"What's your name?"

"Call me Mercy," she says.

Mary gives baby Jesus a bath. She notices that after the bath his temperature seems to go down. She breastfeeds him and lays him down to sleep. Joseph, on the other hand, has been talking to the men of the family and some neighbours as well.

As Joseph sees and learns, Mostorod seems a lovely place to be living and the people are very friendly and welcoming. They offer Joseph and his family a home among them after he explains that they need a place to stay. Some of the neighbours bring them clothes and food. They make their home up for them and set them up among them.

Joseph says he's a travelling craft man and he moves his family along with him every time, wherever he finds work. The people show pity and tell him the danger of travelling too often with a family.

"You need to stay in one place," says Ruffel, Mercy's husband. "Settle in one place and raise your children. What will you do when you have two or more children?"

"I hope I will have settled down by then," Joseph says.

The community is made up of seven houses within a large compound. They have spaces for children to run around and they raise animals. Goats and chickens roam within the court-yard.

Ruffel jokes with Joseph often about settling down in one place while they remain in the community. This gets Joseph thinking about how much he must give to a son who is not his own before he can raise his own. He grumbles with God and becomes impatient.

"Joseph, settle down in one place," Ruffel says when they meet, which is often.

But Joseph is always busy in the courtyard building one thing or another. They've been among them for a week when Mercy and her husband Ruffel walk in.

"We know your baby is a special child," she says. "Now tell us everything so we'll know how to help."

Mary who is holding baby Jesus, almost drops him. She can't believe her ears and it's then she notices that his temperature has completely gone. She's been bathing him in the bathing bowl in the front courtyard for the past seven days, three times a day. He doesn't eat much, but he will take a bit of breast milk and then go to sleep. This already has Mary worried, and now this happens.

She looks at Mercy and silently prays.

"God don't let these be the ones who will sell us out to our enemies."

"I want to know the truth," Mercy insists. "Or you can explain the balsam flowers outside in the courtyard growing within a day after you got here."

Apparently, she had been throwing baby Jesus's bath water away in the same spot in their courtyard, and balsam flowers have grown in the spot. Mary already knows this before Mercy tells her. She knows somebody is bound to find out soon. People will always find her son. She knows he can't hide away from people. Signs and wonders are bound to follow him, and so will people because they read signs and follow wonders.

Mary realizes she must tell Mercy the truth somehow. She

only hopes she's a friend as she seems to be. So, she tells the truth about their journey.

"A mad king is in our kingdom and he's killing every new-born baby," she says. "He's looking for my son to kill him as well. That's why we're running everywhere."

"We've heard of King Herod's massacre," Mercy says. "Many Jews travel past here and tell us the story. Don't worry, you'll be safe among us. We'll watch out for you, won't we Ruffel?" she asks, nudging her husband.

"Definitely we will," replies Ruffel. "This whole town will watch out for you."

Baby Jesus's temperature goes away, and they remain in Mostorod another two weeks. Baby Jesus starts to crawl up to a table or chair and pulls himself up to stand. Mary notices that he doesn't crawl unnecessarily. He only crawls when he wants to get something or stand up. She watches him so often that she becomes absorbed with him. He says a word at times, to mean a whole sentence.

At near to six months old, he starts to stand up and say a word of a sentence. He says "mama" and often points up and says "papa." Mary finds this peculiar. How does he know that heaven is up there at his age and his father is up there? Things seems to go on well among the Egyptians in Mostorod for a while until one day in their sixth week there, Mercy runs inside.

"You must go now," she says. "Run. Take your baby and run. Go up north."

"Why?" Joseph asks.

"Many Jewish spies are coming here from Babylon. They've reached Matariyah and will soon be here," Ruffel explains.

Joseph asks many more questions to be sure they're telling the truth. They seem honest with all their responses and he believes them. Although he has been planning to go southward, now that plan seems foiled. He can't possibly continue southward now.

That night he moves his family out of Mostorod and heads up north where they've been coming from. He decides not to head towards Belbeis, instead he decides to take a round route. They travel towards the Nile and up north they go again. That way they will pass Belbeis without touching the town.

Chapter 6

LEARNING TO WALK

They travel past Belbeis, far away from the town. They reach the town of Tel Basta five days after they left Mostorod. Of course, they rest in caves all along the way. Joseph is thinking they have two days or less before the spies coming from Cairo catch up with them. So, he's wasting no time at all even though he realizes they need to rest often, especially baby Jesus.

On reaching Tel Basta, they find a lot of people gathering about. They're all in a festive mood with foods and drinks being served. It feels like a nice group to mingle with as they find their way around town. Joseph finds a man watching the dancers in the street.

"What's the occasion here?" He asks.

"It's Wepet Renpet and sacrifice is made to all the gods of Egypt," says the man.

"How many gods did Egypt have?" asks Joseph.

He is completely flabbergasted. He can see flowers of all colours and shapes hanging all around the street. Singing and dancing are going on as well as eating and drinking. Along the street, statues of different gods of Egypt have been placed all around in places with flowers and wreath of all kinds hanging on them. In front of some statues, food and blood have been shed and shredded all around.

He looks at the man, who happens to be drinking and expects his question to be answered. The man just drunkenly waves his arm around and speaks.

"They're all over the place. Go and see them."

Now baby Jesus is seven and a half months old. He can say a sentence with just a single word or two. He hears what the man says to Joseph as well as Mary. Mary can't believe they have statues of gods and worship them. It's forbidden by law where she comes from and it's a complete surprise to her.

Baby Jesus isn't surprised. His face turns red. He doesn't cry or anything, but he looks mean for a baby.

"Mama, get down," he says.

Mary is so engrossed in the scene going on in the street that she doesn't hear him the first time. Baby Jesus persists with his demand.

"Mama, get down," he repeats.

Mary finally hears.

"Sorry, love. Do you want to get down?"

Baby Jesus nods his head, and Mary undoes the wrap she has around him. She knows he's been standing and pulling himself up, holding on to things. She sets him down on his feet, and baby Jesus stands there looking furious.

"What's wrong, sweetheart?" Mary asks, seeing the look on his face.

Baby Jesus doesn't answer. He stands straight up and takes his first step. Mary shouts with joy.

"Joseph, Joseph look. He took his first step," she calls.

Many people seem to get interested as well, because they turn and look at baby Jesus standing there, preparing to take another step. Mary claps her hand and walks farther away from him.

"Come on Isa, walk to Mama," she says.

Baby Jesus makes another go at it, his face looking furious. A look of determination is on his face, as well as of fury. He takes his next step and follows with another.

People start to notice baby Jesus as he takes his staggard steps towards his mother. All the statues standing nearby and far away fall over one by one as baby Jesus takes his steps towards his mother. People look to see what's causing the destruction. Some realize that baby Jesus has something to do with it. They watch him take his steps and then they watch as a statue falls to the ground without anybody touching it.

"It's that baby," someone shouts.

"Don't let him walk again. He's cursing our gods," more people say.

Mary walks to her son and lifts him off the floor.

"He's only a baby," she says. "Your gods must be false."

"Who is that boy," asks a man who happens to be a priest of one of the gods. "Bring him here."

People try to snatch baby Jesus from Mary's arms.

"Give us that child," they say.

"Joseph, help," Mary cries.

Joseph comes to her aid, pushing people back from Mary.

"People, if your gods be true gods, why then would a small baby like this affect them? Really, you people should rethink your options. Serve a true God and you'll be saved."

"What rubbish is he speaking? The gods of Egypt are true gods. They live."

"Then let my boy walk through your street, and you can pick up the pieces of your gods," Joseph says.

The priest raises a cacophony.

"We must respect our gods. Oh Egypt, rise and kill these who disrespect your gods. Seize these people."

Immediately, Joseph grabs Mary and pulls her through the crowd, running at full throttle with baby Jesus in his arms. They're ahead of the people, who chase after them. A large fire falls from heaven and casts a barrier between the people and the holy family. The people chasing them can't bridge the fire and the holy family gets away.

Joseph looks back and sees the fire burning fervently, preventing the people from passing through. He wants to stop but his good judgement keeps him running. He realizes that the people coming after them before will have a reason to keep pursuing them. They will know they're on the right path if they hear what happened in Tel Basta.

He decides to put more distance between them and their pursuers. They travel up north for another day before he suggests they should rest.

Chapter 7

ALWAYS A STEP AHEAD

Now baby Jesus is walking and saying short sentences. His baby teeth are out and he's eating solid food at eight months. Their journey pattern, having to run and being chased by people seems to make baby Jesus curious. His forehead crinkles and his eyes narrow. At first, he can't understand why they must run from people.

Mary notices this at their night stopover in a cave. They're near the small town of Meniet Samannoud. She puts him down to sleep after a bath. Baby Jesus refuses to eat. He refuses everything offered to him and walks to the bed Joseph made for him when they reached the cave as he always does. He sits on the bed and talks to himself for a long time.

Mary watches him closely and sees that he's talking as well as listening. She's surprised to see an eight month old who couldn't make a complete sentence having a full conversation with someone. She walks closer and hears him say.

"Yes, I understand."

"Isa, what did you say?" She asks.

He doesn't repeat what he said but points upward.

"Papa," he says.

"Who are you talking to?" Mary asks.

She should've known who he means, but to know for sure, she asks again.

"Isa, who are you talking to?"

"Father," baby Jesus says, then lays down his head.

A few minutes later he's sound asleep. Mary tells Joseph what she learned about Jesus that night before they go to sleep.

"He talks to God all the time, Joseph," she says.

"How do you know that?" Joseph asks. "You mean God is here."

"I don't know. Look, I'm not a prophet. All I know is that Isa talks to him."

"Is he a prophet then?"

"He's more than a prophet. He's the son of God."

"Just because the angel tells you that," Joseph adds sceptically.

"Are you doubting the word of the angel of God now, Joseph?"

"No," Joseph says instantly. "Of course not. I just want to know if you know that for sure."

"What a way to go about it then. Why don't you just ask me directly?"

"I'm sorry my dear," Joseph says. "What I mean to say is did you know that for sure in your knowing."

"Ha, Joseph. How else would I get pregnant without sleeping with a man. God put him there of course."

"You didn't feel anything like someone sleeping with you."

"I'm still a virgin. I haven't slept with a man yet."

"Should we do it?" Joseph asks.

"I don't know, Joseph. This place seems the last place I want to lose my virginity in. Don't get me wrong. Of course, I'm with the right man, but the place and situation are not at all pleasant."

Joseph thinks of Mary as she lies besides him. He thinks of her long, velvet dark hair and her oval face with her bright eyes shining like the morning star. He wonders how on earth he can ever let go off her, though he remembers that he'd wanted to let go before, when he discovered she was pregnant. He now thinks that was a rash judgement and silently thanks God for his angel. *If not for the angel of God I would have lost the woman of my life.* She's just beautifully made and perfectly designed.

As he thinks of Mary his manhood rises. Then, he thinks about the laws of the Jews because he knows if he had followed the Jewish law, Mary would be stoned, having been pregnant before her marriage. He thinks then says softly.

"Laws are not perfect."

Mary heard him and asked.

"What did you mean?"

Meanwhile, Joseph is concerned about his manhood rising to erection that he doesn't hear Mary.

"Mary, I want my own kid."

Mary goes silent for a while.

"Joseph, we have a kid."

"That's God's child, Mary. We need our own child."

"But we can't do anything about it now."

"Yes, we can. I want you right here, right now."

"Joseph, at least be decent. Choose a more decent place."

"We won't get any more decent than this. Believe me woman, we're going to be like this for a long time."

"For how long, Joseph?"

"I don't know. The point is that we should use the time and place we have. We might not be allowed a more decent place for a long time."

"Why won't we?" Mary is getting worried about the insecurity of their fate.

"That's not the point, Mary," Joseph says noticing her worries. "The point is that we should do whatever we can for the present. We can start our family. Like have more kids."

Mary breathes out.

"What do you want from me?"

"I want to sleep with you now," he says. "I can't bear to wait anymore, because the thought of losing you to somebody else is painful. Having you beside me each day and not doing anything is painful as well. Don't you feel lonely or anything?"

"I do, Joseph. But the situation is just that. . ."

"Stop blaming the situation. Let's do it."

"It would wake the baby."

"Not as long as you don't shout."

He leans closer to her and tickles her before he kisses her on the neck. She lets him. After all, she's married to him legally. He kisses her and she falls into his arms before they pull the blanket over them while the fire burns away.

Baby Jesus is sleeping soundly and doesn't wake up. After two hours of good love making Joseph gets up while Mary sleeps. He grabs his trouser and pulls it on, then steps outside the cave. It's a bright clear night and the stillness of the night penetrates the dark, heavy and soundless as it is. The stars in the sky above him play a twinkle melody with their brightness. It just seems a magical rhythm the way the stars shine and dim their brightness.

He feels at peace now that he has finally been with Mary. He thinks back how long since he'd been waiting to sleep with her and the pain he'd endured before the angel put his mind at rest. He'd married her as the angel said but since then he'd put his passion on hold thinking he would be with her when the time is right.

No time is better than the present. He smiles at his good fortune and winning judgement. Mary couldn't resist him anymore.

He feels proud of himself for marrying and sleeping with a virgin, which is customary for a Jewish man. He does more planning of their route before he goes back to sleep, only to wake up again at crack of dawn.

Joseph thinks their chasers will be looking for them throughout the eastern regions, so he leads his family into Meniet Samannoud.

The town is large with large houses and temples. The residents are mostly fishermen who use the Nile to do their fishing, but they're not too accommodating to strangers. They have a long stretch of the Nile running parallel to the town. The holy family walks across the town to the edge of the Nile, where they board a boat and cross the river. By midday they're across the Nile and in the city of Samannoud in the delta area.

The city is very warm, and Joseph feels at peace there. The people of the city greet them as they walk past. The traders are doing their best to get you to buy. Baby Jesus is awake strapped to Mary's chest and looking everywhere as they walk the street. Not knowing anyone doesn't seem to be a problem for Joseph. He seems to have grabbed the pros and cons of being on the move all the time.

He leaves Mary and baby Jesus under a shady tree and walks away to find accommodation. The first man Joseph approaches offers them somewhere to live. He returns to Mary and speaks.

"This place is lovely and they're friendly. I think we should be safe here. Let's stay here for a while."

Mary doesn't complain, as long as she has a place or a home to raise her child. She's happy, something that unfortunately she's been denied since the birth of baby Jesus. She agrees with Joseph, and they settle in Samanoud City. It isn't meant to be a long stay because they're still cautious of their chasers.

By now baby Jesus is beginning to realize that something is wrong with their movement every time. He listens in on his parents' conversations but says nothing, just continues with his own business. During their journeys he has not been allowed to walk but always remain strapped to Mary. So, when they arrive in Samannoud City, he's glad and speaks.

"Mama, city."

"Yes Isa, it's a city," Mary says.

The city is large with big houses and early industries where they make leathers and parchments on an industrial scale. They have a large fishing industry close to the Nile as well. The city is boosting with trade. The city also houses a large pyramid in the southern edge towards the desert.

Baby Jesus is looking everywhere and seems amused by what he sees, such as the small children playing darts and chess game on the floor. He notices the girls play in groups away from the boys. Joseph takes the family to the accommodations he found. It might have been a barn before but has been converted into a cottage. Joseph starts work on it immediately, crafting wood to build demarcation and divide the place into rooms.

He makes beds and chairs with tables before they receive blankets and sheets from the neighbours. They are also given food stuffs as well as spices and oil. Joseph builds a trench for Mary to do her kneading in. They settle in like a normal family and all their Jewish culture begins to come out as Mary prepares more Jewish food.

Joseph finds work at a boat yard, building boats. He makes friends with his fellow crafts men working at the yard. When he gets home in the evening, he does more work on their house. Things seem to be going well and they're enjoying a normal family life. Baby Jesus is growing every day. Mary never stops telling him where home is and that one day, they will return there.

Baby Jesus realizes that they're running away from a mad man who's killing babies. Of-course baby Jesus is only nine months old; Mary is counting down the days to his first birthday.

"Isa, you're going to be one year old in four months," she says.

"Will I have a celebration?" baby Jesus asks.

"I don't know where we're going to be then," Mary says. "Where do you want to do your birthday?"

"I don't want a celebration, mama."

"All right, you won't have a celebration. But why?"

Baby Jesus doesn't have a reason. He just says he doesn't want a celebration. Mary doesn't like that idea at all. It troubles her thinking if it is because of how they've been moving around. She thinks about the money as well but thinks baby Jesus won't know what money is at that age. That night he lies in his bed in his separate room, which Joseph has cut off from the rest of the barn with another room for him and Mary, before he leaves a large area of the barn for living space.

Mary uses part of the living area and the outside space to pre-pare food. Mary lets him go to sleep after saying goodnight with a kiss. She feels proud of him and relieved that he understands their situation.

"Isa doesn't want a celebration for his birthday," she says to Joseph, as they lie in bed.

"You're talking about that already. How are you sure we won't be travelling then?"

"I just think it's a good idea for him to know. I mean, he will have something to look forward to."

"So, what does he want then?" Joseph asks.

"He didn't say. I think he doesn't want a celebration because he thinks we can't afford it."

"Now, tell me Mary," Joseph says. "How can a nine-months-old baby grab that sort of wild idea? Where did you get that from? He's rather too young to understand where we are."

"I tell him every time," Mary says.

In the morning things go on as usual. Joseph goes off to work and baby Jesus is at home with Mary, who is cleaning and preparing food. They've been in Samanoud City for two months, and they've gotten to know a few people around the area. Especially Dahlla, their landlord, and his family. They live in the big house in the courtyard.

During the afternoon Mary takes baby Jesus to the big house to play with Dahlla's little ones. When they reach there, Dahlla is in the middle of a family crisis. Apparently, his little daughter has taken ill, and he has lot of people in the house including doctors. The doctors think the child will die.

When Mary hears about it, she puts baby Jesus down in the room to talk with Dahlla and gives him her condolences. Baby Jesus must have heard what the people were talking about, because he walks to the bed where they laid the sick child and gently places a finger on the girl's palm. Instantly the girl opens her eyes and looks at baby Jesus. She smiles to him and speaks.

"Thank you." Then she looks around the room and shouts. "Papa I'm well."

"What happened? How did it happen?" The people around want to know, and she tells them.

"This baby touched me, and I got well."

Everyone is talking about the miracle healing, and it spreads into the city that a wonder baby heals with a touch. However, while Mary and baby Jesus are at the house, a group of people are coming off the boat into Samannoud City. Joseph gets to hear about it at work.

"Joe," calls Baba, a craftsman from Meneit Samannoud, the next city across the river. "What is going on these days? You know as I was coming on the boat today, I met a group of tourists saying they're looking for a holy baby. They boarded the boat with me with some of them staying behind in Meneit Samannoud."

"Who are these people? Did you see who they are?" Joseph asks. He stops what he's doing, to start packing his bag.

"I think they must be Jews. They didn't do well with the local language,' says Baba.

"Thanks so much, Baba," Joseph says leaving the boat yard at once.

"Thanks, for what?' Baba shouts after him.

But Joseph didn't respond because he's far from earshot. He's running out of the courtyard towards home. Somehow, the four men who landed in Samanoud City that morning don't have luck till later that afternoon, when they meet people coming from Dahlla's house. They told them of the miracle done by a small child and the four men race towards the house. They carry a small blade they keep tucked into their girdles.

They approach Dahlla's house and ask people, who lead them to Mary's cottage. The four men approach Mary in front of the cottage and speak.

"Well wishes to the mother of the holy one."

Mary looks up in surprise. She would have bolted out of the house if her son had not been sleeping inside. After the miracle work, Mary had brought her son straight home to remove him from intrusive eyes. On reaching home baby Jesus went straight to sleep.

Mary is preparing food for dinner when the four men walk in on her. She knows immediately they're Jews. She doesn't think anyone around here would address her like that. But to avoid being obvious, she asks.

"Do I know you from somewhere?"

"No," says one of the men. "We're travellers and come to give you some news. Should we go inside to discuss it?"

Suppose they're angels of God. Mary thinks and speaks. "Do you need a drink? Let me go inside and fetch you some drink. We can sit out here and talk."

Mary walks inside to fetch them a drink as she'd promised. However, on turning back she finds the four men blocking the doorway. One of them walks to her and grabs hold of her covering her mouth in the process. Another stuffs a cloth into her mouth, gagging her before they tie her to a chair.

Afterward, they look around the cottage for the baby and find him sleeping in his bed. The one who finds him walks out to call the others.

"I've found the baby," he says.

"Where is he then? Bring him out and let's go."

"No, you come and carry him," replies the one.

So, the first one stays out of the room with Mary in the living area. The others go in to find baby Jesus. At once three of the men are standing beside baby Jesus's bed. They would reach out to carry him then withdraw their arms again.

"You carry him," one says.

"No, you carry him," says another.

"Or should we just kill him?" says the third one, drawing out his dagger.

"He wants him alive."

"Why? He had all the other babies killed," says another.

"I think this is the one he actually wants."

"Then carry him and let's get out of here."

They reach out for baby Jesus again, only to withdraw their hand repeatedly saying.

"I can't carry him. Maybe you should try."

These three men are stuck in indecision for a long time until Joseph arrives with some men from the neighbourhood who told him that some men were in his cottage with his wife and baby. It's like an invincible shield is blocking them from reaching baby Jesus. They continue to argue among themselves.

Joseph arrives in the front room with five men from the neighbourhood and finds one of the intruders standing behind Mary. They beat him and free Mary before they go into baby Jesus's room to find the others. They beat the four of them and chase them out of the compound. Mary wakes baby Jesus and gathers their things together.

She knows what Joseph will do, once he finishes talking with the neighbours. Joseph spends some time thanking the neighbours for their help even though he knows it will be their last night in the city. He'd made up his mind to take his family away before leaving work at the boat yard. That night they leave the city, with Joseph taking them across towards the northern edge of Egypt.

Chapter 8

HEROD'S SICKNESS

King Herod is sick of one thing. He can't stop killing. His insecurity has grown to a treacherous stage, and his officials know this. Most of them are frightened for their lives and the fear is what pushes them to do his evil biddings.

Namhiba, Herod's chief foreign minister to Egypt, is picked up from his house early in the morning and taken into an underground room below the palace. There, Herod joins them, and he questions Namhiba. In the room is a table with tools like a butcher set. From the ceiling hangs about five swords in their scabbards.

"Tell me, Namhiba,' says King Herod. "As my senior foreign affairs minister, what's your priority?"

"To make you look good abroad, Your Highness."

"And."

"To do your biddings."

"Then, tell me, why did your men find the holy child, but not take him?"

"I don't know, Your Highness." Namhiba says with a shaky voice. "They said they're afraid of God."

"What has God got to do with it? Your men failed me. You are to be punished for it, as it has been brought to my attention that you and the holy child are planning together to take my throne from me."

"That can't be possible, Your Highness."

"Why can't it? Your men found the child, I was told. But they let them go again."

"Not like that, Your Highness," Namhiba says, now really frightened for his life.

"Then correct me and tell me why you still fail to succeed at this mission though I appointed you almost a year ago."

Herod grabs hold of one of the swords that hangs down from the ceiling in the room. He pokes it through Namhiba's stomach. The man screams while blood flows out of him.

"How does that feel now traitor," Herod says. "If you can't do a job, you could at least admit to it and not waste my time."

Herod walks around him in the chair he's strapped to. With the sword still in his hand he takes his time while Namhiba is crying in pain.

"I didn't do anything wrong," Namhiba says.

"Who says you did nothing wrong? Where is the holy child? Why did your men refuse to capture him?" Herod says. Then he pokes him with the sword again before he puts the sword through his left shoulder. He rips the sword out and Namhiba screams out again.

"Now the truth." Herod says. "Do you want my throne or not? Are you working with the holy child or not?"

"You told me to find him. That's what I'm doing." Namhiba says, spitting out blood as he speaks.

Namhiba doesn't notice that he removed the title Your Highness from his sentence but Herod does.

"See, he can't call me his king anymore because he's planning to take my throne."

Of course, after Herod arranged the death of his first wife and two sons for plotting to take the throne from him, most of Herod's officials fear for their lives. None of them dare to rebuke him or confront him for his wrong doings. On this day Namhiba looks into Herod's eyes. Maybe because he knows he will die anyway, still in pain, he looks up into Herod's eyes.

"You're an evil man," Namhiba says. "You send us on your evil errands, and we go and do them for you. You're not good for Judea."

Herod listens to him. Once he'd finish speaking, Herod lifts the sword up and sends it through his heart. He pierces him so deep that you can see a hole in his chest.

"Die, you bloody traitor," Herod says. He pulls the sword back out, dripping with Namhiba's blood. Namhiba looks up for the last time and speaks.

"You're a sick man." He drops his head and gives up the ghost.

Herod drops the sword and calls in two guards. The words Namhiba said didn't even penetrate his skin, much less his heart. He walks out, and on his way out he says to the two guards.

"Get rid of his body. The traitor wouldn't confess."

Herod walks away from the scene of his crime and walks into his throne room. The death of Namhiba passes with only a silent mourning. Nobody dares to confront him or challenge him because since he'd killed his own wife and two sons the council believes that's the end of it.

Any living man that kills his own sons and wife for a throne has definitely lost the concept of a family life. He has gone to the ultimate level of devilishness. A devil cannot conceive the concept of a family life. They fail woefully at it because of the love, the sharing and commitment involved in having a family life. Who is safe from King Herod? Apparently, nobody. Nobody at all is safe and they all know it. On reaching his throne room, King Herod calls a guard and tells them whom to summon. He's been thinking of the man once he left the underground and scene of his crime.

Godwin Osaho, a man from Jericho arrives, looking tall and gallant with long brown hair. He's known to have made his money ripping people off, but in the service of the king he's very honoured. He is rough looking with a high temper and an ego that boasts of cruelty.

"Godwin Osaho, you're definitely the man for this job." Herod says and beckons him to approach. "A post is open in my service. I think it will suit you. You're the man for the job."

Godwin allows himself a grin but says nothing. Just like everyone else, he knows what King Herod is like. He knows the danger involved in working for him and the reward as well. Either way, a king's word cannot go undelivered.

"I want you to fill the post of my foreign affairs minister in Egypt," Herod says. He waits, giving Godwin time to digest the news. Then he says jovially with a smile. "How do you like it?"

"I like it, Your Highness," Godwin says then asks. "What must I do?"

Herod coughs and sits right back on his throne. Then he says.

"There's a mission going on in Egypt now. The holy child is believed to be in Egypt. They've seen him there, but the stupid men fail to capture him."

"So, you want me to capture a holy child."

"He's not just a holy child," Herod says. "They said, he's going to become the king of the Jews, which means he's going to take my throne. God forbid. Any soul who dares try my throne will face my sword. Kidnap the child and bring him to me."

"So, you don't want us to kill him."

"I want it done in my presence, so I can be sure he's dead."

"But, if I may ask, Your Highness." Godwin says looking worried and confused. "How exactly did you say you heard about this holy child becoming the king of the Jews?"

"Three wise men came into my palace thinking the child is here. What a mistake they made but that's for my benefit. They came from far with gifts for him."

"But are you sure about this, Your Highness?"

"I've investigated and it has been confirmed that a holy child was born in Bethlehem."

"You've killed all the new- born babies in Bethlehem. How did they escape?" Godwin says.

"Yes, I did but somehow, they managed to escape. They're found in Egypt."

"But, what about the pharaoh in Egypt?" Godwin asks.

"I will send you with gifts for Pharoah Tutuhkamu and he should give you permission to do what you need to do."

Godwin Osaho is appointed as foreign affairs minister to Egypt just like that, and his assignment is to capture the holy child in Egypt.

∽ *Chapter 9* ∼

FIRST BIRTHDAY

Leaving Samannoud City behind, the holy family journeys northward. Joseph has mixed feelings. He just wants to take his family away from the havoc. So, without clear idea of where they're going, they head north. Again, wanting to put more distance between them and their chasers, he didn't let them stop too much.

They end up spending nights in caves and leaving the next morning. Anyone who knows them and knows what the holy child can do would be able to notice their path. Every cave they stop at hardly has any water, since the areas is desert land. But water just appears miraculously each morning for them to wash and drink. The belief Joseph had in Samanoud City that it was safe is suddenly washed away. In its' place is the self- known assurance, that no place is safe for them.

On their fifth day of travelling, they reach the city of Sakha in the northern delta area. Mary is weary, and her legs can't take another step. She worries about baby Jesus's first birthday since she has been counting down the days. Even though baby Jesus said that he doesn't want a celebration, she thinks it's not right because since he was born, he'd not had a celebration.

It's customary for Jews to celebrate the birth of a newly born baby on the eighth day, which they've not been able to do for baby Jesus. She feels guilty and bothered like it's her fault and she wants to celebrate his birthday.

"Can't we stay here for a while to celebrate Isa's first birthday?" She asks.

"But that's weeks away," Joseph says.

"Only two weeks now."

"In those two weeks, do you know where we could've gotten and how far these people would have travelled to catch up with us?" says Joseph angrily.

"Don't get angry with me," Mary says. "I was just concerned about Isa."

"Birthday celebrations are not an issue now when life and death are a concern," Joseph says.

Without thinking he walks away to find a place for them to stay, though he's not in total agreement with it. He finds a small barn down a country lane and brings them there. The place is far from the road and up against a hill. Joseph doesn't see any water nearby, but he isn't worried about that because God always provides for them.

On reaching there Mary and baby Jesus walk up the hill for a look. Baby Jesus places his feet on the rock. When his feet touch the rock, it sinks in, melting the rock and leaving his footprint behind. Mary quickly pulls him back, and baby Jesus stares at his footprint in the rock.

"That's your footprint on the rock," Mary says when he keeps looking at it.

He looks at his feet and then tries to put it on the spot again. Mary holds him back in fear that the rock might melt too much under his feet. She touches the rock after the print of her baby appears on it and feels how hard it is. Nevertheless, her baby's feet soften it. She puts baby Jesus down by the entrance into the barn to go inside and check it out.

It's good that the shock Mary felt after the attack is wearing off. The journey has weaned some of the horror out of her. Nevertheless, she remains ever cautious and vigilant. She stands at the entrance and looks in the barn where Joseph is busy setting thing up and turning the barn into a cottage. By the time she turns back to baby Jesus, there's a deep well filled with water in front of him. She does a double check in her mind before she says to herself.

"Oh, why do I bother? He dug a well."

She carries him into the barn to announce to Joseph.

"Joseph we've got water."

"Where?" Joseph asks.

"He dug a well just outside the entrance."

After the barn is ready for them to live in, they now think of food. Mary walks up unto the hill towards evening and finds many nests of wild geese. She picks some of the eggs and even a goose she takes down the hill with her. She also finds wheat growing freely which she picks to make flour for dough.

Joseph walks into Sakha city every morning to hear the news and what's going on. He listens to people talking and manages to make friends with some shop owners. Sakha is a city built with pyramids surrounding it. The residents are builders and architects with a few scholars among them.

After two weeks of being in the city and feeding on wild geese and bread they prepare for baby Jesus's first birthday celebration. Joseph has some money on him from the works he'd done in Samannoud City. However, in the only Jewish shop they can find in town they discover that they don't have enough, and they would be destitute if they spend the money, they have on them at the shop.

They remember their last item of worth, which is the last gift the three wise men gave to baby Jesus, the myrrh. This they sell to an embalming shop which values the product and reward them handsomely. They have enough for the birthday celebration and enough to keep on them. At the Jewish shop they purchase everything they need for the celebration in Jewish style. They buy a new tunic and a coat for baby Jesus. Joseph invites some nearby neighbours he'd gotten to know. Two men come with their families.

Mary prepares potato latkes and matzo balls soup with chicken meatballs along with some Jewish brisket, and olives and sliced carrots. She makes a coffee cake kugel with some coconut macaroons and a tray of reuben sandwiches. In all she prepares six different types of Jewish occasional food and has them laid out on a table by the time people are arriving.

Mary is so curious to see baby Jesus mix with other children that she hangs around him throughout the celebration. She also fears somebody will take him away while she's not watching. One family that attends, has a two year old daughter and the other family has two sons who are one and three years old.

Baby Jesus looks at the kids with a curious gaze. It must be hard on him never being able to mix with kids of his own age. The little girl comes to him and holds his hand.

"Adafa is my name," she says.

"Jesus," Baby Jesus says.

Mary, listening to them opens her mouth in surprise. Why did he call himself Jesus? She did name him Jesus as the angel told her, but she has been calling him by his pet name. She didn't think he will know his name. But there he is introducing himself as Jesus.

Adafa holds his hand and smiles girlie to him. They are about to walk away hand in hand when Mary calls him back. She uses his first name not wanting to confuse Adafa.

"Jesus, don't walk away," she says. "Stay with mama."

Baby Jesus can see the fear in her mind. He can tell her heart pounds at every step he takes away from her. Adafa is pulling him so they can go, but seeing his mothers' worry, baby Jesus hesitates. He loosens his hand from Adafa and walks back to his mother.

Adafa sits with him on the floor beside Mary, where they play. The guest don't stay too long and after they leave Mary cleans the cottage and prepares baby Jesus for bed.

Her worry persisted through the night because of the guest that came to baby Jesus's celebration. She worries, one of them will tell their chasers who they are. She questions Joseph that night.

"Joseph, did you think these people are safe?"

"We have to trust somebody, Mary," Joseph says. "We can not go without talking to people, and I'm sure everybody is not the same. We just need to choose wisely who we talk to and trust."

"It's just that that girl was leading Isa outside earlier. I don't know where she was leading him, but my mind wasn't at ease with it, so I called him back."

"Did he listen?"

"Yes, I was surprised. He introduced himself to her as Jesus."

"That's his name."

"Yes, but we don't call him that. How did he know that?"

"You said yourself that he talks to God."

"Oh yes, I see," Mary says then asks. "You mean God told him his name is Jesus?"

"Who else?" Joseph says. "Get some sleep now Mary. We leave in the morning."

"We're leaving so soon?"

"We must. The people from Samannoud City will be coming after us. I don't want a repeat of what happened there."

"They just want my baby. Where else can we go?"

"I've asked around and I'm told if we go north we'll come to the last city there, which is Alexandria, then the great sea. But if we go down to the south, we'll come across many more cities. We can cross the Nile to cover our path more."

"Joseph, aren't you tired of all this walking about from place to place. When is it going to end."

"God set us up on this course. He knows what's best for his son," Joseph says. "That's how I think of it. I don't know what you think."

Mary thinks about it for a while and then she kisses him and turns over to sleep.

"You're right, Joseph. God knows what's best for us."

Chapter 10

IN THE WESTERN DESERT

Early the next morning, Joseph prepares for the journey. He packs some provisions and the food left from the cele-bration. Among the provisions are a small tent and a few other items he purchased. He fills three water bags. They set off at an early hour, taking the southern route.

They're almost out of town when they meet a trader selling camels. Joseph approaches the man and offers all the money he has on him for a camel.

"Please. This is all I have on me," Joseph says after hearing the price of the camels and donkeys.

He realizes he doesn't have enough to even buy the smallest donkey. "I need a camel to go into the desert with my family."

The man looks at Joseph and then beyond him to Mary and baby Jesus standing a distance away. He smiles a mischievous smile knowing that's the reason he pitched his shop here, for these people going into the desert. He knows they'll pay more for the last resort they can find. He looks at his animals then says.

"For that amount I can give you that one over there." He points to a small and thin camel.

The camel looks haggard and deprived, which makes Joseph wonder.

"*How far will this carry us before it dies?*" Nevertheless, he pays the man all the money he has on him. Having been told about the journey ahead, he knows a camel will help get them through the desert. He puts their provisions together and ties them to the camel, then he sits Mary and baby Jesus on the animal while he leads it on foot. The journey is rough and weary. The desert sun beats down on them with a biting tendency and yet they continue.

On the first night they have to camp on the desert sand right in the middle of nowhere. They pitch their tent and camp for the night, hills of pyramids surrounding them, on every side. They eat from their provisions and drink before they sleep. Joseph knowns that, in the desert he will have no place to find wood for a bed, so he packed enough for them. In the tent, there's enough blankets and pillows to sleep on.

First thing in the morning, Joseph packs everything away and they set off again. By now baby Jesus is walking and he's grown his front two teeth, so he's not nursing anymore. He's eating what Mary gives him and the third water bag is for him to drink from. His talking isn't fluent yet. Since Mary and Joseph speak Aramaic to each other he's picking up on the language little by little.

While they journey on, Mary tells baby Jesus stories of Egypt especially the ones the Jewish are commanded to remember. Such as when they receive the Ten Commandments and when they're led out of Egypt. Baby Jesus doesn't ask questions but listens. Mary isn't sure if he takes in what she says to him. Most times, he seems to be far away somewhere in his mind as they go along.

They rested on the second night in the desert and feed on their provisions. They feed the camel as well which runs low their provisions and Joseph realizes they won't have anything for the third night if they don't make it into a town. Mary is worried but baby Jesus doesn't look bothered at all. He enjoys sitting in the sun and drawing in the sand with his hand whenever they stop.

By the third night, they still haven't reached a settlement. They must camp in the desert, and of course they have nothing to eat and drink. Joseph set up the tent and waits. Mary asks.

"What are you waiting for?"

"We need to eat and feed the baby," Joseph says, "I'm waiting on God."

Mary goes back into the tent. When she lies down, baby Jesus lies beside her. Soon a strong sandstorm rises in the distance, and it can be seen coming towards them. Joseph rushes in and tells them to get up.

"We need to run now. There's a sandstorm coming towards us," he says.

Mary grabs baby Jesus and follows Joseph out of the tent. Sand is everywhere, blowing in the air. There's no air to breathe in just sand. They leave their tent and everything they have and look for a safe place. They haven't gone far from their tent when the storm becomes heavy around them. They can't see anything, even baby Jesus.

Mary and Joseph shield him to get through the storm. It's all around them and their path is completely blocked by the ragging storm. Baby Jesus, still in Mary's arms stretches an arm forward and shouts.

"Stop."

Immediately the raging sandstorm stops, with the sand settling down to earth. The air is clear and even their tent is intact. When they look around, there are large birds laying on the desert floor. They're flapping their wings to take off but can't because they were caught in the storm. Joseph sees them and instantly gives thanks.

As the darkness falls, Joseph sees what looks like flat loaves on the desert floor. He picks one and eats it before he gives thanks and picks more. He still hasn't cut the bird because there's no water and he just wait. He takes the loaves in to Mary and baby Jesus.

"There's no means to cure the bird. There's no water."

"Let's wait on the Lord," Mary says.

Baby Jesus gets up like he's heard a command, with a loaf in his hand, and walks out of the tent. He stands outside for a second or two just watching and listening, then bend down and scoops the sand from the earth. Water comes up through the sand and he yells.

"Mama water. Come see water."

Mary and Joseph see the water and are amaze that even the desert swells with water for him.

"Why do we wait for God?" Joseph says. "When we have him with us here."

Mary turns the words around in her head.

"Isa only does what God tells him to do," she says.

Joseph cuts and washes the bird then roasts it on an open fire. They eat and rest for the night. In the morning, they start again, packing their stuff on the camel and setting off into the sunrise. On the fifth day they reach a settlement which is known as Al-Asqeet. There's hardly any other building in the area except for one with pyramids on the edge of the settlement.

There are about three sites with new buildings being built, and they appear to be camel farmers, because they have about three pens with lots of camels in them, both young and old. People are living out of tents in a large settlement.

The settlement has a ruler who has the only erect building in the area. It is a large building spanning a wide courtyard. The ruler is a large man, tall with a long white beard. His face is rough looking, with dark patches from healed bruises. Somehow, they have no standing statue of a god. He welcomes them and allows them to pitch their tent in the settlement.

Joseph notices, they appear to be pyramid builders because he can see their tools laid out within the settlement. He sees hammers, shovel, scrappers and lots of self-made sand-bags. They pitch their tent and baby Jesus goes outside the tent to play. He sits on the sand and doodles on the ground, drawing large lines. Then he writes words down on the ground, that even Mary or Joseph can't pronounce.

When evening comes baby Jesus walks behind their tent and makes water swell out of the ground. He digs a large area around the water where he can sit and bath himself. He sits in the water and splashes. Their tent is in the middle of the settlement where Mangore, the ruler directed them.

"Pitch your tent here," he says. "Here I can watch over you."

Mary thinks that's what he says to every new arrival, so her worries fall away. She yearns to put her feet down and go to sleep. She feels safety is around her and then hopes to pursue her leisure moments. They've explained briefly to Mangore, the chief that they have enemies looking for them without going into full detail. They are not sure if he believes them, Mary is glad they found a resting place.

Joseph is worried and nursing a fear inside him. The fear comes when he remembers Mary tied to a chair in Samannoud City. He still hasn't got rid of it. It's like every time he sees her, he panics because he remembers. Each day they spend in Al-Asqeet, he's filled with anxiety to move on again. He's frightened that a repeat of what happened then will happen again. Even though the people in the settlement are friendly and welcoming, and Mangore vows to protect them, Joseph doesn't feel at all secure. He's counting everyday they spend around the settlement as another day for their chasers to catch up with them. Joseph considers their options and knows they must keep moving.

It's King Herod that wants baby Jesus dead. Joseph can't possibly confront the king. or raise a war against him. It's one man against a large force. He can't do much around the settlement because there's hardly anything he can do with sands which is all they have. Joseph doesn't want to learn to build a pyramid. The area has a large and deep well they draw water from, but they also use the water baby Jesus brought up from the ground. When Mary wakes up and finds baby Jesus already washed and in clean clothes, she is amazed.

"Did you wash Isa and dress him?" She asks Joseph.

"No, I didn't," Joseph says. "I saw him in the back washing in a pool. I thought you put him there."

"I've been sleeping, sweetheart."

Both walk out of the tent with suspicious looks on their faces. They seem to know what is going to happen. When they reach behind their tent, they find the pool but with balsam flowers in different colours all around the area. Mary and Joseph know this is a trademark. It will cause others to be curious. There's no way to hide it. When the locals see the flowers, they say among themselves.

"Surely, he must be from God."

They are hallowed and more affectionate towards them, offering them gifts to pray for them. They even kneel before baby Jesus saying he should lay hands on them.

"God is with you." they says.

With this going on, Joseph feels more threatened and prepares for them to leave. They set off from Al-Asqeet on the seventh day. Having fed their camel and watered it well, they set for far in the western desert.

For days they don't reach another settlement, travelling for miles on foot and a camel. They did rest for nights, where they find water and fill their bottle. They pack enough food and water to last them another two or three days.

The harsh hot sun of the desert beats against them, making them run thirsty so often that they run out of water. They don't have a map, so figuring their location is guess work most of the time. They've been travelling in the desert for four days before Joseph says.

"I think I can feel water."

"Water, where?" Mary asks from behind on the camel. She's been singing to baby Jesus, and Joseph joins in at times.

"I think it's a river," he says looking eastward at the horizon.

They rest for the night on the spot and pitch their tent. In the middle of the night, they can't sleep because flies enter the tent. Miraculously they fly around baby Jesus where he sleeps, but none of them land on him. They just fly around him and then away. But there's so many of them that Mary and Joseph get worried and use a cloth to sweep them all out of the tent.

In the morning they leave early, before the sun comes out. They travel east for another four days before they finally come to the Nile.

Chapter 11

ACROSS THE NILE

"I told you I can feel a river," Joseph says happily.

"But that's four days ago," Mary says. "By the way how can you tell?"

"It's in the wind and the cloudy sky around the river," Joseph says. "It travels for a long distance, and you can tell."

They travel along the Nile for a while until they find a boat to cross the river. Joseph thinks if they cross the river to the other side their chasers will lose track of them in the desert. Joseph walks to a trader and barters for the sale of the camel.

It's no surprise that the camel has put on more weight. It has built up to a strong animal by the time Joseph wants to sell it. He sells it for a high return, twice the amount he'd bought it for which makes him happy. With this thinking and some change in hand Joseph takes his family across the river. There's a chance they can rest a long time if they can find a welcoming community.

Crossing the Nile in a canoe is star-studded scenery for baby Jesus. He watches the river with awesome attention.

"Mama, mama, water," he says. And spreads his arms wide apart to show how big the water is. "Big water, mama."

Mary smiles and smooths his hair. His hair is a long jet-black colour taking after his mother. His slightly pointed nose is also like Mary's. She smooths his hair again.

"If the Nile River amazes you, Isa. I wonder what you'll be like when you see the great sea."

Baby Jesus is watching the water flow. He's so excited that he wants to touch the water. He reaches out and bends over the edge of the canoe. Mary has her arm wrapped around him to stop him from falling into the water.

Once they've crossed the river into Matariyah, they travel away from the river and go through the town until they reach the southern edge. Matariyah is a small town and less than a hundred miles away from Cairo. The town is rich with large houses. It appears to be a town where the rich come to retire, and things seem a bit expensive. But the people are very friendly and welcoming, greeting them and offering them drinks.

"Come and join us," they say.

Joseph knows it might be rude to refuse for no good reason. He takes them in, and they drink wine with them before they continue on their way. At one or two places, the resident brings out food and asks them to share. Once they've eaten, they continue their journey after explaining that they must keep up with their travel plan. Joseph realizes these people are good to be among, but he feels it's unsafe for baby Jesus. He notices they do a lot of drinking and feasting on a regular basis. They're not cautious of any danger which in a way is a good way to live your life but with what they are going through, he knows they can't just live among them.

They find accommodation with a man named Mustafa, a Jewish shop owner. He rents his house out to scholars in Ain Shams and Matariyah alike, and he's able to rent them a room. Joseph paid for a week at a time. They eventually spend three months there. By the time they move in, baby Jesus is trying to express himself verbally. He looks at the house and says to his mother.

"Mama, house." He points.

"Yes, Isa," Mary says. "It's a house and this is where we're staying for a while."

After Joseph settles with his landlord, he sets about making a bed for baby Jesus.

"Won't it be better if you go and buy one for him?" Mary says.

"That will be wasting money that we don't have," Joseph says. "I've always built his bed. It's my duty. I'll soon be finished."

"Then you'll have to make our own," she says.

"Yes. Don't worry, I'll have everything ready by bedtime."

Mary goes about making the place homely for them. She kneads dough and makes dinner ready, while baby Jesus plays around the house. He doesn't have much to play with and with the boiling sun pouring out on them he soon gets bored and agitated. He walks to the front courtyard where Mary is busy preparing the meal.

"What's the problem Isa?" Mary asks seeing him looking worried and bothered.

"Tree," he says.

"Tree?" Mary asks curiously. She looks around them in the courtyard and sees no tree. She wonders where he gets it from.

"I want tree," baby Jesus says.

This is about his first complete sentence. Mary runs to where Joseph is working around the corner.

"Isa said his first sentence," she says.

"But the boy talks," Joseph replies.

"No," Mary says. "He actually said 'I want tree.'"

"Give him a tree then," Joseph says and Mary laughs.

She walks back around the corner to the house. In the court-yard a tree is growing big while baby Jesus stands by and watches. When he sees his mother, he says.

"Mama, tree."

"What did you do?" Mary asks, but she already knows the answer.

While she stands there the tree grows into a large fully grown one and baby Jesus walks under it and sits. It's shady and cool under the tree and that's where he plays every day. When most of their neighbours see the tree, it becomes the talk of the town. Everyone is coming to see a tree that grows in a day. Nobody talks to them about how it happened, and Mary and Joseph prefer not to draw attention to themselves.

That same day, baby Jesus makes a spring of water in the courtyard. It's like a well deep enough for him to stand in and wash. As soon as he finishes his wash, balsam flowers of all kinds of colours grow all along the pool of water. The courtyard is changed within a day, and it too becomes the talk of the town.

The scholars living with them invite their colleagues and they discuss the tree that grows in a day and the wonder baby. They soon become the thing everyone is talking about, and people love them wherever they go in the town. But with all this atten-tion Joseph worries and he's ever on the lookout for anyone suspicious.

Joseph gets a job, working for a building site. He earns good money but still works at home in his spare times. Near the Nile they're building a new set of houses and Joseph works there. He's working on top of a building three months later when he spots some men on the street. He notices the three men stopping people walking by and asking them questions. He doesn't hear the questions, but his suspicion rises like a dragons' bare teeth.

He senses danger and instantly leaves work and heads home.

He takes a different route to the men and reaches home faster because he guesses someone will point them out soon. Mary is preparing the evening meal while baby Jesus is in the courtyard under the tree listening to the discussion the scholars are having there. Joseph calls Mary inside and tells her what he saw.

"Did you question them?" Mary wants to know.

"No, but I can smell danger."

"Joseph, we can't possibly run again without a good reason," Mary insists.

"Mary, you don't need an angel to tell you when danger is around," Joseph says. "I can see them asking people questions and that's enough for me. Let's go now. Go get the baby and let's get going."

Reluctantly Mary walks back outside to fetch baby Jesus. He's outside touching everyone there and saying.

"You're blessed."

Mary's getting comfortable here and doesn't want to leave. When she picks up baby Jesus, he takes one look at her and says nothing. Mary is so preoccupied with the thought of having to get on the road again, she pays little attention to baby Jesus even when she picks him up and he lays his little hand on her head and says.

"Bless you, too, mama."

Joseph is already packing all they need for the journey. He packs their tent, one bag and some food for the night before they set off that evening. Joseph walks to Mustafa and pays him what he owes before he takes his family out of town again. Taking the southern route, they cross into Ain Shams and continue south-ward towards Babylon, the old Cairo.

Chapter 12

IN BABYLON, OLD CAIRO

Leaving Matariyah and Ain Shams behind, they travel on for hours, walking over hills and along mountain paths. Good thing it's the evening and the night soon comes on them. Travelling through the night is a problem, especially with a toddler.

They stop for the night in a cave under a mountain. Baby Jesus's bed is gathered leaves and fallen tree branches that Joseph makes into a bed for him like a nest. Like always, in the morning they have food and water to wash before they set out again, walking through valley and low land in the scorching sun. They soon get weary but that afternoon, they enter Babylon, old Cairo. This isn't the capital city at the time. The capital is still far away on the western desert edge of the Nile.

Babylon is an important city, though, and the city is in a festive mood when the holy family arrives. The festival of Iris is going on and street parties are everywhere. The main street of the city is lined with statues of different gods of Egypt. Baby Jesus takes offence, and yells in frustration.

"Mama, down, I want to get down."

"Isa, there's too many people around. You can't walk here."

Baby Jesus is not having it. His eyes are teary and he struggles with her until she feels it's rather impossible to carry him. Mary looks at her son and she can see the look on his face. It frightens her because she's seen that look of anger on his face before. She sets him down and holds his hand and they continue to walk. But with every step baby Jesus takes, an idol or statue falls to the ground in ruin.

This keeps happening as they walk along, and people start to notice. Curiously they watch the little toddler walking and then see their statues fall and crash to the ground. He doesn't turn to look at the statues but walks straight ahead. Mary and Joseph follow him. Joseph knows that this is trouble.

Mary and Joseph walk on either side of baby Jesus with Joseph carrying their luggage. Soon, people approach them, and stop them in their tracks. Baby Jesus wants to walk on, but Mary grabs him to stop him.

"Isa these people want to talk to us because they're angry," Mary says.

Baby Jesus looks at the people around them and looks at his mother, then says.

"God is angry with them. Is that why they're angry?"

"No, Isa. It's because of their idols."

"That's why father is angry."

Mary is quite amazed by his talking that she forgets about the people around them. Joseph talks to the people. A man, he's tall and lanky with a body posture that swells with authority speaks.

"Your child must come to the governor with us."

"Why?" Joseph asks. "He's only a child and I'm sure he meant no harm."

"He's ruined our festival," someone shouts. The others agree with one accord.

"He's only walking."

"Then come and show the governor how he walks," they say.

They push them toward the road and when baby Jesus starts walking, they see the rest of their standing idols, crash down. They're overwhelmed and angry at the same time.

"How did he do it?" They ask.

"Who's your son? What's his name?" Some others ask.

Mary quickly grabs hold of Joseph's hand nudging him not to tell them. He understands her fear and says nothing to them until they reach a large temple, and they're pushed inside. Of course the place is filled with statues decorated in different colours of flowers.

Baby Jesus steps in, and the statues fall one by one with every step he takes. This doesn't amuse him. His face looks furious which worries Mary. She thinks that she's got a real trouble-maker here. If he is doing this at just eighteen months, what will he do when he becomes a teenager?

Joseph on the other hand is praying softly to God. He knows the trouble they're in and knows they will need a miracle to get out of this. The crowd of people follows them into the temple and only stops when the holy family stops. They're standing in front of the governor and top officials of the city. Mary and Joseph are aware of the trouble they're in, but baby Jesus just wants to continue walking because he can see more statues still standing. Mary picks him up and he speaks.

"Mama no, leave me alone."

"Leave the kid alone," says a man standing up from the chairs where the governors are sitting. He walks towards them. "Leave the child alone and let's see what he wants."

Mary puts baby Jesus down and he walks away from her. With every step he takes, a statue falls, until only one statue remains behind the governors' seats. The governors are furious and yell at the top of their voice.

"Who's this kid?"

"Where is he from?"

"Seize them now and stop that child from walking."

"Yes, he shouldn't walk again," the people agree.

Mary runs to her son and picks him up into her arms.

"Isa you've made these men angry," she says. "They're going to arrest us."

The man standing in front of them is the foreign affair minister to Egypt. He then says.

"Don't worry, they can't touch you since you're not Egyptian. I will stand for you, and they can send you back to Judea. Even I will come with you."

Mary and Joseph think fast.

"How did you know we're from Judea," Joseph says. "What's your name?"

"I'm Godwin, the foreign minister of Judea to Egypt," he says. "Have you thought of bringing this child up in his hometown. It's my job to know all my citizens."

"So, you work for Herod," Mary says.

"I'm just doing you a favour," Godwin says. "You can take it or deal with these people yourselves."

Joseph realizes the trouble they're in. He knows that Godwin is not just Herod's man. He's here to take them to Herod himself, where they will put baby Jesus to death. Staying behind in their current situation isn't looking all that great either. *These people will want to stone us to death or sacrifice us to their gods. They look malevolent and eager to tear us apart because of the statues. Something they can build again.*

Joseph has been praying softly. Now he looks at them and speaks.

"All of you want the son of God, don't you? You want to arrest him for destroying your statues. If you're serving a living God, he won't be angry with you, but your gods are false."

At this, the high priest of Iris, who is standing close to the governors raises his voice and speaks.

"Be gone with them. They have brought shame to the temple of Iris and to all gods of Egypt. They must be put to death. Seize the child and his parents. Guards," he calls.

The crowd rushes towards them, Mary holding baby Jesus looks to him and say.

"Isa we're in trouble what can you do to help?"

"Take them. Take the child," says the high priest.

"Do you want my help now?" Godwin says.

Joseph and Mary say nothing. Nevertheless, Godwin turns to the governor.

"High priest, governor and the people of Babylon," Godwin says. "I'm Godwin the foreign affairs minister for Judea. These people are foreigners and strangers among you. They do not know your customs and ways. If you hand them over to me now, I shall see to it that they're returned to Judea and removed from Egypt."

"Are you strangers in Egypt?" The governor asks.

"But we're not going back to Judea," Mary says.

"Then you choose to be sacrificed to Iris. You and your child," the high priest says.

Godwin smiles.

"I hope you get what you want. Because Herod is getting what he wants either way."

"Oh, you cruel man," Mary says.

"Arrest them, guard," the governor and the high priest say.

The guards approach the holy family, but before they can touch them, a massive lightening bolt rips through the building and finds the high priest. The high priest is thrown against the last standing statue, and it falls on him crushing him to death.

All the people are in awe. They look with awful gazes, seeming stupefied. They are afraid to touch the holy family. Even the guards are looking bewildered, and terror seizes them all as they stare at the high priest. It's like the lightening flash temporarily rendered them blind.

During all this a voice is screaming in Joseph's head "Run, run. Run." The voice keeps saying. While everyone is still looking terrified, he grabs baby Jesus from Mary, holds on to her hand and runs out of the temple. The people don't see anything. They're all just staring blindly.

Racing full throttle out of the temple, they turn towards the city exit. They're far in the distance when Joseph looks back and sees men chasing them. They are not the Egyptians, but Jews, and his guess is that Godwin has sent men after them.

He continues to run, and doesn't stop until they reach the outskirts of the city. They turn southward and continue to run. When they reach the outskirt of the city, they stop and look back again but don't see the men again. They don't assume they've lost them but found a hidden place to stay for the night.

⧼Ѹ⧽ Chapter 13 ⧼ѻ⧽

OUT OF HARM'S REACH

Old Cairo wasn't a pleasant place for the holy family. Joseph and Mary agree that they should run as far as they can. They want to get far away from the rowdy crowd. But the Jews that Godwin sent after them worry them because they don't know how far they will go to find them. Joseph stops and thinks. *"Haven't they been the same Herod's men chasing us since they reached Egypt. Godwin is in on it as well."* Joseph is so sure of it that it frightens him. With the sort of influence Godwin has among the Egyptians it could only mean trouble for them. He explains this to Mary as they walk on.

"Whatever you decide, Joseph," Mary says. "I know God is with you."

They walk into Maadi in the middle of the night. Maadi is only about ten kilometres away from Babylon, old Cairo down the southern end. They couldn't find a place in Maadi in the night, so they walk through town until they reach the southern end.

A mountain looms in the distance away from the road. Joseph goes straight for it and on reaching the mountain finds a small cave under it. He goes in and investigates first before he takes his family in. They stay in the cave for two more days. They'd left Babylon without any provisions for themselves. All their bags and provisions had been left behind. However, they have themselves and that's enough sometimes.

But God doesn't leave them without, because early the next morning when they wake up the mountain is covered with a fog. When the fog clears, at midday, they find birds and loaves spread out on the mountain. This continues until the third day. Meanwhile, baby Jesus makes a spring of water gush out of the mountain by just touching it.

"Water," he says, tapping the rock while Mary watches.

To her amazement a spring of water gushes out of the mountain side, and he dips his hands in it and washes his face. For a small boy of just eighteen months, he's pretty much a genius. Mary observes as his confidence grows and silently offers praise to God. She's sometimes lost in her wonder at what her baby can do. He's managed to surprise her on most occasions. But she knows he has a teacher beside him teaching him what to do.

On the third day of their stay in the cave Joseph comes up to Mary and speaks.

"We should leave in the morning."

"Why again?" Mary says. "Can't we rest here more?"

"You've rested here more than enough," Joseph says. "Soon this mountain will be filled with people once your son's mojo gets loose."

Mary opens her mouth and can't close it. What surprises her is that Joseph has been paying attention to things she hasn't considered. He's right, baby Jesus's mojo is the crowd he draws along with him anywhere he goes. Crowds just come from nowhere and they will be wondering what Jesus has done.

She eventually agrees with Joseph, so early the next morning they prepare to leave the cave. They set off on their journey when they suddenly meet a group of people heading to the mountain.

"Hello there," calls out somebody from the group of five adults and three children. "Is God still on the mountain?"

Joseph stops at these words. He and Mary look at each other before looking at baby Jesus in Mary's wrap, then back at the mountain. A dense cloud rises from the mountain and into the sky.

"What's that cloud?" everyone in the group is asking.

Even Joseph and Mary can't explain it. They just turn back and walk away from the group as quickly as they can.

"Let's go up the mountain and see," someone says from the group. They all run up to the mountain while Mary and Joseph walk away with baby Jesus.

They reach the road and set southward when a small group, a man a woman and two children stop them.

"Please friend, are you coming from the mountain?" The man asks.

"Which mountain are you talking about?" Joseph says.

"That mountain of course," the man points. "I can see the glory of God there."

"I'm afraid you'll have to go and find out yourself."

"Won't you come with us?"

"Thank you so much," Joseph says. "But we must go now."

Joseph and his family walk away from them, with the other family looking at them as if they've gone insane by not coming to the mountain with them. They leave the baffled family alone and walk on. They're walking past the river crossing when an idea strikes in Joseph's mind.

"Mary, should we cross the river again into the western desert?" He asks.

"Why cross the river again?" says Mary.

"Herod's men, Mary, remember? They're still after us and I think Godwin is the one seeing to their work here."

"So, he's the one sending men after us."

"Yes, and he takes his orders from Herod directly as the foreign affairs minister."

"So, we can't escape him because he knows the Egyptians," Mary says.

"Let's cross the river and I will explain to you."

They walk down the path to the river and Joseph bargains with a ferry man. With the money on him he pays for their crossing, and they board the ferry. There are lots of people standing or walking around by the ferry crossing. Joseph pays close attention to them all, making sure nobody who looks Jewish is boarding the ferry with them. He leads them to a corner of the ferry where they sit.

For more protection he makes sure to hold on to baby Jesus. They are still on the ferry when Joseph explains to Mary.

"You know quite alright that Herod wants to kill your son and not you."

"Should that give me comfort Joseph," Mary says. "The death of my son is wrong he might as well take me because my son has done nothing wrong."

"What I'm thinking now is that he wants all of us dead and not just the boy anymore."

"What makes you think that?"

"Because of what Godwin said. He said he wants to lead us to Judea himself. Which means to Herod."

"But Herod will just kill the boy and set us free or throw us into jail to die," Mary says. Then thinking again, she says. "What am I saying. None of it is good. I just hope God will do something about him in time because I'm getting weary of this moving around all the time."

Chapter 14

HEROD ON HIS SICK BED

King Herod is in his room, which is large and elegant and fixed with a large golden four- pole bed. The newly besotted queen, Herodine, is sitting at the edge of the bed. King Herod fell sick a week ago after his frenzied party at the palace. He's been with so many women, he can't even remember their names or faces.

Even his wife, Queen Herodine, was confused at the party as to where exactly his love lies. She can't say she's pleased to see him in bed now instead of sitting on his throne. She takes pity on him to see him in this state.

Herod climbs out of bed in his white sleeping gown and lifts it up. Herodine screams immediately. Under Herod's gown his genitals have grown to double their usual size. What's worse is the pus, which is a whitish liquid. She runs out of the room but stops at the door and walks back to Herod, who's looking at himself confused.

"See what happened to you now?" She says. "After that orgy you had at the party, see what happened to you. You're not fit to be a king now. You better call your physicians and sort this out. I can't lie in the same bed with this."

94

Herod cocks his head left and right without taking in what his wife is saying. Then he says.

"Mariam, listen," calling her by her first name. "They're talking again."

"Who's talking?" asks his wife.

"The babies. The children of Judea. They're screaming at me."

"Let them scream," says Herodine. "You can't save them. Look at your own state. God knows you need saving yourself."

Herod manages to dress up while his wife goes on about his state and him being a mental case. He says nothing, and she finds it hard to believe that Herod will take her insult and not say anything in return. They walk out of their bed chamber and into the throne room. As soon as he reaches his throne, he screams.

"He's here. He's here." Herod looks in the distance, away from his throne to where the sunlight shines through the window. "Can't you see him? The holy child."

With a strong will, he sits on his throne.

"You've grown," he says.

In the distance, a flood of light shines into the room from outside. Within the light stands a young boy with a golden crown on his head. His gown is golden. The light shines from him. He looks at King Herod and says nothing. Herodine, sitting next to him on the throne can't see anything,

"Where do you see a child?" She asks.

Herod doesn't bother to answer her but concentrates on the image he's talking to.

"My men will soon catch you."

The boy smiles and points a finger at Herod. Instantly Herod holds on to his ears and screams.

"They're shouting into my ears. Get them to stop," he says.

"Who are they?" Herodine asks.

"Children, lots of children of Judea," he replies.

"But I can't see them," she says.

He looks at her like she has gone mad and then says.

"What about him?" pointing to the image of the boy.

Herodine can't see anything.

"There's nothing there, Herod. Nobody at all."

Herod holds on to his head and shouts out.

"I'm going crazy."

"I will call somebody, and you can find a physician for that." she says, pointing down at his genitals.

The image disappears but Herod doesn't feel any better. As they wait for the doctor to show up and he's explaining what's wrong with him to his wife, Godwin shows up, having just arrived from Egypt. He walks down the aisle to the king and Herod looks with surprise.

"Godwin my favourite servant. How's Egypt?" Herod says.

"Egypt is fine, my Lord," Godwin says.

"Have you got the boy with you?"

"Your Highness, I did come in contact with the boy in Babylon," Godwin says then adds. "He's no longer a baby now, my Lord. In fact, he can walk and talk."

"Don't I know that by now?" Herod screams. "What exactly are you telling me? Have you got him or not?"

"No, Your Highness. I haven't got him."

"So, you let him escape again. Is that it?" shouts Herod.

"Your Highness, God is with that boy. You can't touch him."

At these words, Herod grows angry and goes for a sword hanging down beside his throne. He draws the sword and starts to throw it at Godwin but Herodine holds his arm.

"No, Herod, no more killing," she says. "You didn't even consider your state."

But Herod looks on angrily and rises from his throne.

"What is he telling me? I'm Herod the great. There's nobody I can't touch." He beats his chest. "Who's this boy? I want him. Bring him to me."

"Your Highness, I'm sorry but I think I can still get him," Godwin says. "My men are out after him now as we speak."

"Find him," Herod screams. "Find him and bring him to me."

Godwin rises quickly and walks out of the throne room. He walks fast so that it takes him little time to reach the exit. Meanwhile, Herod looks at him hastening away.

"He will betray me as well," he says. "He's a traitor to the throne."

"They're all traitors," Herodine says. "Come and sit down."

Herod walks to his throne and at once collapses on his throne and start screaming.

"What's it?" Herodine asks.

"It hurts. It hurts," he says.

"What hurts?"

He points to his genitals, and she understands.

"Let's go into the bed chamber and wait for the physician."

Herod agrees and tries to rise but he notices that the light shining into the room from the sun is getting brighter and he stops to see. The light gets brighter, and the image of the boy appears within. Herod moves towards the image and his wife calls to him.

"Herod come, let's go inside," his wife says.

Whether he heard her or not, nobody knows, but he continues to walk toward the image until he's a foot away. He raises his finger and speaks.

"My men will find you."

"Who?" Herodine asks from afar.

He pays no attention to her. Before he can say another word, a voice comes from the image of the boy, and the boy speaks.

"I thought you would change. Now I see you're completely evil. There's no human in you. Surely you shall die of that illness."

"What illness?" Herod screams. "It doesn't kill. It can't kill me. You lie. See, I'm fine. You're a liar."

The image disappears at once. Herod stands there for a while before he turns around and sees his wife who has been standing there looking at him.

"Am I going to die?" He asks.

Chapter 15

BACK IN WESTERN DESERT

Arriving in Memphis isn't as glorious an event as they would have liked. From the first look, the city doesn't appear to be a safe haven. The roads are crowded and there's shouting and hailing going on everywhere. Traders and hawkers are throwing banters at each other. The houses are built close together and almost look like the city was planned out except for some few staggered houses on large estates, which tells that the city really wasn't planned out. People just built the way they wanted to. It's meant to be busy. It's the capital city for a reason. It stretches far into the western desert from the shore of the Nile.

Joseph sees what the people had told him was true. He's gained some information about the capital city from their journeys. He knows from hearing that it's no safe place to take refuge.

"Are we staying here?" Mary asks, looking sceptically around.

She knows they could get lost within the crowd, or they could be caught by anyone without them knowing.

"No," Joseph says. "We're going past Memphis to Bahnassa. I've been told that they're building a new city there, so there's lots of work and the place is safe."

"How far away is that now?" Mary asks.

She's worried that she will have to walk more days before

settling down. Mary is getting home sick. She longs for her house in Galilee and walking up and down in Egypt is wearing her out. She doesn't want to argue too much or make complain, knowing it's for the safety of her son.

"About two to three days away," Joseph says. "I've got some money left on me. Can we see what it can get us for the journey ahead?"

They walk around the market and buy a tent, a camel and few items for their journey before they set off, taking the western route which takes them deep into the desert.

By the first night they've left Memphis behind and are in the desert, walking in the desert sand. It's not easy walking on sand because it's like walking on the beach. With every step the leg sinks into the sand and lifting it up for another forward pace takes effort.

Of course baby Jesus is strapped to Mary's chest on the camel. He does fall asleep sometimes during the journey but in the boiling heat of the desert sleeping is quite hard. However, in the evening when the sun goes down, the weather cools down the earth around them. They camp for the first night in the desert, pitching their tent on the sand and lighting a campfire to heat food up to eat before they finally settle in for the night.

Baby Jesus falls asleep because the coolness of the evening makes him tired. They stay for two more nights in the desert before they finally reach Bahnassa on the fourth day. The city is deep in the desert and like Joseph expected, the area is just being developed. Lots of houses are being built and roads laid out.

They find a place in the city and pitch their tent. Joseph goes out to find work at a building site. They live out of their tent for about two weeks until one day Joseph comes back from work and takes them to a house. It's not much, just a single bedroom to share with others.

They settle in but being back in a house and living with other people has impact on baby Jesus. Having people around him seems to make him happy because for most of their journey he's often quiet. He quickly makes friends with the neighbours, and they all like him. They buy him stuff on their way from work or trade and later in the evening everyone gathers with the neighbours in their courtyard and listen to stories from an adult.

Somehow, the group in the courtyard gets bigger daily. More people from the neighbourhood join them. Even travellers stop by. Baby Jesus gets to share his opinion about God with the crowd. He knows how to move the crowd with his words, and they all gasp sometimes.

"God is our father," he says, and the people around look at him in wonder. Then he adds. "He loves us," with a cheerful attitude.

"How can a child speak with such words?" They ask themselves.

He becomes a favourite among the neighbours. Nobody realizes that he's drawing in more people. But Mary and Joseph know so they're ever vigilant towards baby Jesus. The crowd in the courtyard continues to grow, Mary gets worried.

"Joseph, he's doing it again."

"He's doing what?"

"Did you see the crowd in the courtyard this evening?" Mary says when they're getting ready to sleep.

"I noticed but I thought they're just neighbours."

"It's his mojo," Mary says. "He's drawing them here."

"He's not doing anything spectacular," says Joseph.

"The crowd is getting bigger. It's like they're waiting for him to do something."

"Just watch him closely and make sure he doesn't do anything serious," Joseph says.

Joseph is getting comfortable at his job. He's growing to like the city because it offers everything they need, especially with a Jewish shop in town.

"It's like we've finally found our haven," he says to Mary.

"In this desert city," Mary says with a dislike.

"Mary don't be displeased. Look soon your son will grow up and defend himself. We can now start planning for the future. Please, be happy."

"Wait, Joseph," Mary says "When you said plan for the future what are you talking about?"

"Oh, come on, Mary. You're not stopping with Isa alone. I want more kids."

"But Isa is still a baby," Mary says to make excuses because she knows baby Jesus is no more a baby.

He's a toddler with the mind of a teenager. But while she talks, Joseph moves closer and grabs her in an embrace. He kisses her and she eventually returns his kisses. They make love and forget about baby Jesus drawing the crowd.

Soon, an event happens that causes Mary much concern. Evening is approaching and baby Jesus is in the front courtyard with Mary. He's helping take things in and out of their room, which Mary sends him within the house. As he's coming from inside the house a man is walking past, baby Jesus fixes this man with a concentrated gaze. The man walks with a limp in his right leg, and he carries a heavy load on his back that makes him bend over.

Baby Jesus walks to the edge of the wall and stands there watching the man. As the man tries to walk past him, struggling with his load and his limp, baby Jesus smiles at him and reaches out with his hand to the man. When the man reaches him, he stops and speaks.

"Hello little one."

"Touch," baby Jesus says, since the man is not close enough to touch him.

The man moves closer and takes his little hand. Instantly the man's leg straightens out and his colour changes to brightness. The man laughs and looks at baby Jesus.

"You're a magical one," The man says.

Meanwhile, Mary is kneading dough. When she sees that the man is still there talking to her son, she goes to fetch him.

"Is this your son?" The man asks.

"Yes. Why?" Mary asks looking at the man curiously.

"He just healed me from my paralysis."

As they talk people gather around them. The man continues to tell the crowd what baby Jesus did for him.

"He healed me," he says.

Mary instantly carries baby Jesus inside. She finishes making the dinner and then waits till Joseph gets home. She doesn't let baby Jesus out again into the courtyard until Joseph gets home and she tells him.

"What do you want me to do now?" Joseph says.

"Is that all you can say?" Mary asks, her anger showing. "I told you he healed a man. Can't you see what that means?"

"No, Mary, we're not going anywhere yet."

"Usually, I'm the one saying that. Why are you saying that now?"

"Look, Mary," Joseph says. "We've been here for four months now, and it feels safe. Don't you feel safe here."

"Well, I did, but now I'm beginning to feel unsafe."

"Let's wait and see, then we'll decide on what to do."

That's what they did. The following morning Joseph goes off to work. During the day Mary gets loads of visitors. The man baby Jesus healed comes back with a gift and more people who need healing. They all come with lots of gifts and expecting to be healed.

Mary gets so angry that she takes baby Jesus inside and refuses to let him out. Baby Jesus gets angry with his mother shouting.

"Mama out. Mama, I want to go out."

"No, Isa, you can't go out," she says.

Baby Jesus walks to the door and bangs on it, shouting.

"Mama, I want out."

"Isa" Mary calls, "you can't go out to these people. They would drain you of everything you have and leave you with their junk they call gifts."

"No, Mama," he shouts. "I want to go out."

"Well, you can't go out. It's got to be my way today," Mary says and walks away.

When Joseph arrives, she tells him. He's already seen the camp the people are making around them outside. When Mary tells him what happened, he agrees with her.

That night while the people are still camping outside their house, the holy family packs up and leaves Bahnassa. They take the southward route until they're outside the boundary of the city before they stop to rest for the night.

Chapter 16

A COMMON HAVEN

On the first night they stop to rest after leaving Bahnassa, baby Jesus is somehow confused about why they had to leave their home again. He was just getting used to being among people, which is why he was angry at his mother. This is the first time Mary hears his opinion, and it worries her. Baby Jesus before he goes off to sleep in the tent asks.

"Mama, why did we leave home?"

Mary is at first shocked then gives herself a minute to breathe.

"To keep you safe, Isa," she says.

"Why?" baby Jesus ask. Mary has no direct answer to give him.

She doesn't want to go into the story of why they left their original home in Judea to come to Egypt. She thinks he won't be able to assimilate the story yet so she says.

"In time Isa, you will understand." She kisses him. "Now get some sleep we have a long journey ahead of us tomorrow."

Mary realizes he refers to Bahnassa as home, their little bedroom there which he'd grown accustomed to. It hurts her that her child must grow up wandering about in a foreign land, and not be able to settle down and live his childhood.

She also thinks about what sort of responsibility awaits him.

She thinks he knows what he must do already and he's just waiting until it's his time to act. She remembers the anger he threw at her when she didn't want him to go out to the crowd. She just hopes they will wait till he's grown up before they began to task him with their problems.

Mary thinks all this through before she falls asleep that night. She doesn't discuss much with Joseph in the night. Not because she doesn't want to share her thoughts but whenever they're camping in the tent baby Jesus is often sleeping in between them and they can't have privacy. Not that they can do anything anyway. They're often so tired from their journey that they make their bed and fall asleep to wake up refreshed in the morning.

The following morning however she gets to see another side of her son. As they're packing up and getting ready to go baby Jesus asks Joseph a question.

"My father won't be running away every time, Joseph," he says. "Why are you running?"

Joseph stops folding the tent away and looks at him for a long time before he says.

"Well, God set us on this road."

"Did he?" Baby Jesus says. "Why didn't I know then?"

"You were just born then," Joseph says.

"Oh, I see," baby Jesus says. "That's why I didn't know."

Joseph can't believe he's carrying on a conversation with a two- years old, like he would with an adult. Baby Jesus has only two weeks left before his second birthday. They had been thinking they would celebrate it in Bahnassa. As things turned out, they had to leave.

As they set off, continuing their journey southward, Joseph ponders over his conversation with baby Jesus as he leads the camel. He realizes baby Jesus calls him by his name and refers to

God as his father. He marvels at how he knows that and what's different in how baby Jesus knows God compared with how they know God.

They stop two more nights before they finally reach a new city, the city of Samalout. Far in the western desert the city of Samalout is just rising, with lots of construction and new buildings. Seeing this makes Joseph happy and he thinks it would be the same as Bahanassa. They find a safe place to pitch their tent, and for the first week they live out of the tent. Joseph goes and gets a job at the building site and a week later he moves them into a house for baby Jesus's second birthday.

Joseph is happy to stay in Samalout because he finds work, but after baby Jesus's second birthday, he gets worried, not because of anything spectacular but because he has learned from what had happened to them in the past. He wants to be more ahead of their chasers. He talks it out with Mary, and they even share it with baby Jesus.

"We're leaving tomorrow." Joseph announces two weeks after baby Jesus's second birthday.

He has just arrived from work and feels uneasy when he enters the house. The house is a converted barn that he renovated himself, turning it into a living space with a bedroom for him and Mary and a separate room for baby Jesus.

"Why again?" Baby Jesus asks.

He gets up from the table and walks into his room without finishing his meal.

Mary and Joseph watch him walk away. Joseph realizes they need to explain to him fully what's going on and why they need to be moving.

"You need to explain to him," he says to Mary.

"Why do we have to leave so soon?" Mary asks him.

"I feel we need to keep moving," he says. "I notice the longer we stay at a place, that's when trouble starts. These people after us are still coming. So, we're better off moving than staying too long. This city is not that safe."

"When did you decide that?" Mary asks sensing there's trouble already and Joseph is not saying it.

"I see lots of people coming off the ferry and coming into the city. We can't keep track on who is who among the crowd coming in. I think we better keep moving."

Mary relaxes and breathes out. She's glad there's no immediate trouble, just a precaution he wants to keep. She agrees.

"Isa, I want to talk to you," she says, walking into his room. He's lying on his bed looking up to the roof. He sits up facing his mother.

"What did you want to say, mama?"

"I know you're angry that we must leave again, but you must understand why. That's why I want to talk to you."

Baby Jesus says nothing but looks her in the eye to show he's listening. Mary talks at length, telling him what happened when he was born and how the angel of God appeared to Joseph and told him to go to Egypt.

"Isa, that bad man is still alive and searching every day to harm you. We must keep you safe from him."

After she finishes, she watches him as he says nothing. His face is lowered, looking at a spot on the bed. Mary thinks maybe he didn't understand her. But the thought hasn't left her mind when he looks up and speaks.

"The wicked shall perish in their ways, mama."

Mary realizes that he did understand her quite well.

"You're right, Isa," she says. "It's the wickedness they will do before they perish that we're trying to avoid now."

"I understand," he says.

"Now, get some sleep. We have a long journey tomorrow."

They leave the following morning. Joseph wakes up with a new idea to avoid the chasers. He suggests they cross the Nile. So, from Samalout they cross the Nile into Gabal El Tair.

CO Chapter 17 CO

THE DESERT DUST

Gabal El Tair does not prove to be as a welcoming place for the holy family as Joseph had hoped. Apart from having to resort to live in a cave Joseph couldn't find work and he didn't like that idea. They reach across the Nile by late afternoon when the sun is still harsh. And, baby Jesus decides to walk the instant they get off the boat.

"Mama, I will walk," he says, coming off the boat.

"It's a long way sweetie. Would you rather have mama carry you?" Mary says.

Joseph is walking ahead with their simple luggage. Mary holds on to baby Jesus's little hand, and they walk behind Joseph. Already Joseph is getting agitated because he doesn't see any building site around. What they see are giant buildings that were built in ancient times.

They walk along the street finding no place to rest, pitch a tent, or even rent a room. If the townspeople were welcoming at least one person would have invited them inside by now, away from the hot sun. All this is going on in Joseph's head as they walk the street. At last, as it turns evening, he gets fed up and leads his family away from the city towards the mountain. He finds a cave at the base of a mountain and decides they should stay here. Inside the cave is so dark that he struggles to light a lamp. He finds moss and wraps it around a stick but he has no fire. Striking two stones together to make fire seems an endless task until baby Jesus comes closer.

"What are you doing?" He asks.

"I'm trying to make fire. We need fire to see inside the cave." Joseph explains.

"Fire," baby Jesus says.

Instantly flame lights on the stick Joseph's holding. He doesn't at first think it's baby Jesus who makes the fire. He thinks it's the stones he's striking together and speaks.

"Well done me. I did it. I make fire."

But Mary who's watching them closely from behind says.

"No Joseph, you didn't make that fire. Isa did."

Joseph stops as he's going into the cave with the lamp in his hand.

"What did you mean Isa made the fire? I cracked the stones together."

"He commanded the fire," Mary says.

"All right, I've heard it all," Joseph walks into the cave with the lamp in his hand.

Baby Jesus and Mary walk in after him.

"What's this place, mama?" baby Jesus asks.

"This is where we'll be living," Joseph says "It's safe enough and not suspicious just as long as you don't draw the crowd here again."

"Joseph, don't blame him. It's not his fault," Mary says.

"I'm not blaming him. I am just saying he doesn't do it again."

"That sounds like a blame to me and you're angry with him."

"No, I'm not," Joseph says.

111

"You mean you don't blame him for having to come to Egypt and wander around a strange kingdom."

"The Lord God set us on this path, Mary," says Joseph. "Surely, I can't blame the child for that."

"Then if a crowd shows up here tomorrow, don't blame him."

Joseph is walking in and out of the cave gathering woods and leaves with branches. He sets about to make a bed for them while Mary tries to find food. They haven't packed any food since they left in a hurry as usual. Mary looks at baby Jesus where he stands at the entrance into the cave.

Baby Jesus bends down and scribbles on the ground. Mary is still thinking about how they will find food. She's thinking of asking baby Jesus to do something but again she thinks about it and says.

"No, he's too young. He won't even understand."

Then she turns around and looks at the cave and Joseph still bent over working. He had crafted out a bed for baby Jesus and is working on a larger one for them. Lamps hang around the cave. With that they have a campfire going to warm the cave as well.

Mary in her worries sees the drawing on the ground. Baby Jesus draws a cross on the ground.

"Mama, a cross," he says, pointing to the ground.

Mary moves closer and sees that the cross he draws has somebody hanging on it.

"Isa, is somebody on the cross."

"Yeah." he says, Then he turns and looks at her in the eye. He hugs her and says, "Mama, I love you."

Mary's heart bleeds at once, she grabs hold of him and pulls him closer in a close hug. She's so happy and appreciative as well as stunned, because this is the first time, he has said these words to her.

It sounds like heaven to Mary's ears. Her heart rate goes up and down swelling past its' usual state. She feels so happy and still hugging him she says.

"Isa, God's blessing is on you."

She walks into the field in front of the cave, and her eyes go up to the mountain. She can see birds of various kinds perched in the trees on the mountain. She looks again, then laughs.

"God has provided us with food," she says. She calls baby Jesus saying. "Isa, come with mama let's go and get some dinner to cook."

"From where, mama?" Baby Jesus asks, getting up and following her.

"From the top of the mountain," she says while leading the way.

They follow a rough path to the top of the mountain. As they climb, Mary is picking up birds eggs and dropping them in a cloth she's using as a bag. By the time they reach the top of the mountain she has enough eggs. At the top of the mountain, she finds many birds and manages to catch a sleeping one.

She picks flowers as well to use as spice. When they've climbed down the mountain with their catches, they're tired.

"Mama, I want a drink," baby Jesus says.

"Oh gosh." Mary exclaims. "We haven't found water."

Baby Jesus stops and points to a spot on the rock.

"Mama, water," he exclaims happily.

Mary walks closer and looks, but there's no water there, just rocks sealed together in segment. When she sees there's no water, she's confused because baby Jesus had never lied to her before. Surely, as God's son he can't tell a lie.

"Isa, there's no water here," she says. "Come let's go."

Baby Jesus refuses to move. He stands there with a happy smile.

"Water," he says.

"There's no water there," Mary says. "Look I can't see any water."

"Mama, water." He bends down and lifts a segment of rock. He pries the rock out and water gushes out of the rock. Mary is more than surprised.

"How do you know, Isa?" she says and hugs him.

She goes into the cave to tell Joseph and carries the food in while baby Jesus stays by the spring and plays in the water. By dusk they've eaten and are set for bed. When Mary looks for baby Jesus she finds he's fallen asleep by the campfire where Joseph is telling him about the prophets and the Torah. As Mary lays him into bed, he opens his eyes sleepily, he says.

"Mama. See you in the morning."

"See you in the morning, Isa," Mary says. "And God bless you."

She kisses him on the forehead and draws up the cloths to cover him. Then she walks to the campfire where Joseph is still sitting. He's picked some fruits, guavas and apples. A crunching noise can be heard in the cave as he bites into an apple. Mary sits next to him.

"You know Isa knows things we can't even imagine."

"He's God's son," Joseph says. "I'd expect more from him."

"He finds the water in the rocks easily," Mary says talking on like Joseph hadn't said anything.

Joseph repeats himself.

"He should know. He's God's own son."

"Joseph, will you stop saying that as if that explains every-thing? He's human and a small boy. He's my son and that makes him flesh and not whatever you think."

"I'm just saying," Joseph says. "The world is waiting for him to be king of the Jews."

"Joseph," Mary exclaims. "Why are you like this?"

"I hate this city," Joseph blurts out. "There's no work and we can't find a house."

"Don't be discouraged, Joseph. There's always a silver lining in the sky," Mary says, "Why don't you try tomorrow. Go into city yourself, me and Isa would stay here. Go and look for work and a house we can stay in."

Although grudgingly Joseph accepts, and they go to sleep. Very early the next morning Joseph set out into the city after they've eaten, scrambled eggs and roasted bird. Mary and baby Jesus wait behind in the cave. They have the rest of their roasted bird to eat and more scrambled eggs which baby Jesus likes.

When Joseph returns in the evening, he has no happy news for them. He couldn't find a job or a house for them to live in, but he did buy some provisions they will need. They eat and settle for bed by the campfire. Joseph and Mary take turns talking to baby Jesus about the Torah and Jewish culture which they've learned before their bar Mitzvah. They told him why they need to get married after their bar mitzvah. They told him the story leading to his birth and then they explained to him why they are running around a strange land, even though they've told him some part of it before.

Baby Jesus listens to all this and afterward he only has one thing to say.

"Father's way is perfect."

This they repeat daily after Joseph returns from the city. He still doesn't find work or a house to live in. Days turn into weeks and just two weeks later Joseph gets bored of repeating the same thing every day. He doesn't want to go into the city anymore.

He's thinking of leaving the city completely but still holds it back from Mary.

"Let us all go together today," he says.

Mary sees no reason they can't. She's getting bored of sitting in the cave all day as well, so she agrees, and they all leave for the city taking their few belongings with them.

Baby Jesus is walking between Mary and Joseph as they enter the city. They stop at a shop and walk in. As they go into the shop two men with turbans around their heads and faces wait outside the shop.

"I think it's them," one says.

"Then we must let Godwin know we've found them," says the other. "How are you sure it is them?"

"Jewish family wandering around with a small kid. They fit the description."

"Okay then. Let's go and tell Godwin."

Both of them enter a different shop along the same road. In the shop they confront a man and speak.

"We'll like to send a message to the Jewish foreign minister."

The man looks them up and down before he leads them into an office. They all sit.

'What's your message,' the shop man asks.

"Tell Godwin that we've found the baby and his family in Gabal El Tair here and we're following them."

"Okay, I'll deliver your message," the shop man says and sends them two away.

The two men return to the other shop they saw the holy family enter. They wait outside for a while but when they don't see the holy family, they enter the shop. They question the shop keeper about the family that came into the shop.

"I don't know," the shop keeper says. "They only wanted a room to rent."

"Can you tell they're Jews and did they say where they're going."

"I told you, they only wanted a room to rent," the shop keeper says. "And I don't know where they went."

The two men walk out of the shop and stand on the road outside the shop. One of the men then says.

"If they should escape to another city. We have people there to pick them up."

"It's simply good that Godwin spread us all over Egypt to find them. It's like we will always know where they are and can attack any time we want."

"That's Godwin's plan. He knows how to seek people out."

"We've lost them. They might still be in the city looking for a place to stay."

"Should we go and tell Godwin that we've lost them."

"Let's wait till tomorrow. If we don't find them, then we go and tell him otherwise he might think us stupid."

Meanwhile the holy family has gone onto the next road in search of a place to stay and a possible job for Joseph. After they've walked into many shops and houses, Joseph gives up and speaks.

"Come on Mary, let's get out of this city."

"So soon, where would we go?"

"Anywhere but here," Joseph says. "Look, in two weeks I haven't found a job and I've searched. We can't find a house as well."

"You're losing hope so soon, Joseph," Mary says.

"No Mary, God is not here. So, the sooner we get out of here the better it will be."

They walk into a local restaurant and buy their next meal before they walk to the waterfront. A boat is going out across the river. Joseph says they should get on it.

"This might be our only chance to be free of this place before something drastic happens," he says.

Mary sees no immediate danger, but the idea of having to go back into the cave for another night bores her. Eventually she agrees with Joseph especially when he adds.

"Look, Mary, the safety of Isa is what matters and here in this city I don't feel it."

They leave on the boat setting off across the Nile in the early hour of the evening. The sun is radiant in bright orange as it prepares to slip down the horizon. Baby Jesus has a short nap on Mary's lap while the boat sails away.

Chapter 18

IDOLS FOR GOD

If their last stop at Gabal El Tair proves to be unhospitable and a disappointment to Joseph, their next stop at Al Ashmounein proves completely hostile. After the boat takes them across the Nile, they come to the edge of Samalout. From there, they must walk miles to reach Al-Ashmounein in the southern end of the western desert.

Joseph doesn't want to stay in Samalout anymore and takes them into the desert. First, it's baby Jesus they have to deal with before leaving the boat. He wakes up as the boat is docking and then refuses to leave the boat.

"Isa, we must go before people start to notice us."

"But, mama, it's dangerous there."

"Isa, danger lies everywhere," Mary says. "We just have to be more careful. Come quickly."

Joseph walks back to them, lifts baby Jesus off the boat and carries him down the road along with the luggage. Mary takes the bag from him. They walk out of the city and into the desert taking the southern route. Having thought of this trip on the boat, Joseph buys a camel with other items they may need for the desert journey. Three days in the desert with a hot sun and a warm bed at night. They feed and water their camel regularly for the three days it takes them to reach Al-Ashmounein.

On the third day, seeing the city from afar baby Jesus refuses to go any further. Mary implores him.

"Isa, we've walked for three days to get here. It's no use now turning back."

"Mama, I don't want to go," baby Jesus says.

"Why?" Mary asks. "Will you tell me why?"

"Because it's dangerous there."

Joseph who had been listening to them interrupts and speaks.

"Isa, I can't see any danger here. The only danger is staying longer in this desert."

"Joseph, why do we have to go into this city anyway?" Mary asks, getting worried and concerned.

"Mary, if I remember correctly the word of the Lord is that we will not have gone through Egypt before he visits us again." Joseph says. "The way I see it, if we keep returning to the same city we won't get through Egypt in time."

"But you don't know how long it will take us," Mary says.

"I know it will soon be time," Joseph says. "Look, we won't stay in this city. Let's go through it to the next one."

Mary agrees, and Joseph leads the way on. They walk into the city without looking for a place to pitch a tent or a place to live. They just want to get through it like Joseph had promised. However, unknown to them, the people of Al-Ashmounein love their gods to the extent that they have the idols of their gods all around their city and in important places.

In the city square there's a large statue of Iris standing and gazing at the people of the city. The towering statues look like they're forever gazing at the people in a trance. It's everywhere you turn your head. Baby Jesus asks if he can come down.

"I want to get down," he says.

"Joseph, set him down on his feet," Mary says.

"No," baby Jesus says. He points to the camel and speaks. "On there."

Joseph sets him on the camel while he and Mary walk, pulling the camel along. By the time they come into the city, baby Jesus looks absorbed in his own thinking. And, from him a flow of energy comes out, looking like an electromagnetic force. It passes through the people without harming anyone but once it reaches the standing statues, it splitters them into pieces.

They continue to walk on and the same happens wherever they see a statue standing. They all split into pieces, falling down to the earth. People are running from the falling statues. At the same time, they're looking around for the cause of the commotion.

When they realize that it's their gods only that are being attacked, they get angrier and look around for the cause. However, as things are happening, and the statues fall, Joseph gets cross with baby Jesus. He turns back and stops walking.

"You're doing it again," he says. "Stop it now before we get into trouble."

"Joseph, he can't help it," Mary says. "It's not his fault if these people are not so blind to worship idols for God."

Some of the people heard them and concentrate on them.

"He said the boy is doing it," someone says in the crowd having heard Joseph talking with Mary and baby Jesus.

"Then get them," someone shouts.

"People are looking at us, Joseph," Mary says.

The people come closer to them and one of them asks.

"Is your boy a god?"

"He's the son of God," Mary says. "God of Israel doesn't like idols. That's why he's destroying them."

The people are amazed, but they tell them to keep on moving so they can watch. Joseph walks on again pulling the camel. He hopes baby Jesus won't do it again because he doesn't trust these people.

As they walk on, baby Jesus sees all the standing statues. He releases the force again and all the statues fall, smashing into pieces. The people are angry yet amazed at the little kid knocking over their idols.

"Come to our governor," they say. "You and your kid."

Joseph, remembering what happened in Babylon, refuses and speaks.

"Sorry we can't go. We're just walking through your city. We're going to the next city down south."

"I know who you are," says a man among the people. "Is he not the holy child? Come with us and we'll get you across."

"No, no need," Joseph says. "We know our way. We just want to get through the city. Thank you so much." He quickly leads his family on.

He'd seen the man talking, and he'd noticed two men looking more like Jews than Egyptians, although they dressed like the Egyptians.

As they walk on, the havoc baby Jesus is doing to their idols continues. He doesn't stop until they reach the end of the city, with the people walking them to the city limits. They get angry and shout a lot, with some of them saying.

"Let's stone them to death."

But even though they shout, nobody picks up a stone.

"Go get out of our city. Go, go away." They shout.

As they shout, Joseph continues to walk his family out and

baby Jesus reigns his havoc on them. When they reach the city limit, the people stop and watch them walk away into the desert. They've gone far away before Joseph stops.

"Can't you control yourself, Isa?" He asks. "See the trouble you got us into there."

"I told you it's dangerous here," baby Jesus says.

"Joseph, he said that," Mary says before Joseph says another word. "Remember, he didn't want to come into the city. I think he knew what would happen there."

"You mean he can see the future," Joseph says.

"Yes," Mary says. She walks to her son on the camel and hugs him. "Isa, it's true you said that, but when God set us on this journey, he told us to walk through Egypt. We must go through all these cities."

"All right, mama," baby Jesus says.

Mary joins him on the camel while Joseph walks on leading the camel. They don't stop again until late evening when they pitch their tent in the sand.

CHAPTER 19

A HOME IN THE DESERT

On the first night of their journey from Al-Ashmounein, they camp in the desert with their tent. Two large set of pyramids rise ahead of them in the far distance, while the rest of the area is dusty desert sand.

From the provisions Joseph bought before they reached Al-Ashmounein, they're able to eat and drink and feed the camel. The night goes slowly with the sun setting between the two pyramids.

They would have been able to sleep properly through the night if not for the flies. They're everywhere jumping from surface to surface in the desert sand. Baby Jesus can't sleep nor can Joseph and Mary. By morning, their body is covered with fly bites. Baby Jesus is itching everywhere, scratching till it turns red. So are Mary and Joseph, they're all scratching.

The journey must continue, so they leave early in the morning and set off again. By evening, they all have sore spots on their body and get extremely sick. They stop for the night in the desert, and that's when Mary realizes they've used all their provisions on the way. So, with sore bodies they all lie in their tent, when Mary says.

"Isa, we have no provisions left. No food or drink." She thinks that baby Jesus is old enough to supply their needs.

Baby Jesus can see her frustration. She looks broken hearted, and he knows why.

"Mama, God will provide," he says.

"I could've told her that," Joseph says from where he lies.

Baby Jesus turns to look at Joseph and speaks.

"Yes, you can say that, but do you trust he would do it?"

"What sort of question is that from a two -year- old?" Joseph says and sits up on the mat.

"No, Joseph," Mary says. "He's two and half."

"What difference does that make?" Joseph says. "He's still too young to question my trust in God."

"His age is nothing, Joseph," Mary says. "Don't look at his age."

As the hours go by, they still haven't gotten anything to eat, so they are even more hungry. Together with their itching bodies and sore skin, they soon get very tired. Mary could've shouted at baby Jesus to do something and save himself if not them. She holds her tongue, however, till the last minute when she can't stand it anymore.

The weather is warm as well, so they must take off their clothes to their underwear. Mary starts to walk out of the tent but as she reaches the door, a storm starts with lightning and thunder. The rain pours heavily for twenty minutes then stops.

Mary stands at the tent opening for the whole twenty minutes, thinking to herself *What's the purpose of this rain? What is God doing, and what are they to do with the rain?* She can't figure this out until the rain stops along with the lightning and thunder. Everything is calm and cool.

When the storm stops, Joseph and baby Jesus get up as

well. Mary finds a pool of water behind their tent and further down she finds food in form of fresh wheat sprouting out of the ground. She collects these and makes a meal out of them. She puts baby Jesus in the pool and washes him. Afterward, balsam flowers grow on the edge of the pool. She collects the flowers and makes ointment for their skin.

They spend another three days in the desert regaining their strength to continue their journey. They don't do anything special except to eat and sleep and rub ointment on their bodies. After three days, their skin is clear of all sores and itching. They get up on the third day and continue their journey, reaching Dairout on the evening before night fall.

On entering the city Joseph realizes they can't be looking for a house at this hour of the day anymore. He suggests they go around the city and find a place to pitch their tent. The city looks normal since they didn't have idols, which is Joseph's first concern. Although they have a large pyramid looming over the city.

After his first concern about idols has been laid to rest, he set about to solve the next problem which is finding a place to pitch a tent. The city has lots of large ancient buildings which would have been built during the old pharaoh's rule. They walk around the city for a long time without anyone challenging them until they find a place in a field to pitch their tent. Other tents are pitched around the area with people living in them. It's like a small community of travellers.

There's a spring of water nearby with the children from the community gathered there playing in the water. As it happens it's this same spring that serves as the community's water supply. Having been in the desert a long way, baby Jesus is pleased to see the water. He walks toward it as Joseph and Mary pitch the tent. He finds a bowl and draws water to wash his feet.

Meanwhile, the other kids there are dipping their feet directly into the spring. Baby Jesus doesn't like this idea and he watches the kids splash water and laughs heartily. He likes the idea that they're happy and wishes to do the same, but he realizes that the spring they're dipping their feet into, is the same spring the community is drawing its water supply from. He walks to some of the older kids there sitting close by and speaks.

"You guys are wise, right."

This makes the four older kids look at themselves again and at baby Jesus. They're not more than sixteen years of age. Baby Jesus catches their attention straight away. He isn't finished because he adds.

"See this spring? That's what this community is living on." He shows them a woman drawing water from the spring near the place the kids are dipping their feet.

"Yes," the kids reply. "So what?"

"Now look at the kids there dipping their dirty feet into the spring. They've made the water bad for the woman drawing it down there."

"What's that have to do with me," one of the kids says. The others are still thinking. One says,

"Kid, you've got a good brain. You make a lot of sense."

"What do we do now," asks another of the kids.

"We tell the kids to move down the river and the people drawing can draw from up there."

"Is that good, kid," they all ask baby Jesus. He nods and speaks.

"Do it quickly."

The older kids lead all the kids out of the spring, and direct them further down where they can play. Baby Jesus jumps in the water, splashing and getting himself soaked with them. Mary gets him out of the water and changes him once they've finished setting up.

They have few provisions, but they can stay the night. As the evening turns to night, the children play in the field around the camp with campfires burning. Baby Jesus joins in to listen along with the Egyptian children. This becomes an everyday activity for children to gather around the campfires and listen to stories. Baby Jesus is well happy to join in with the other children.

Their stories are mostly about Egyptian gods and goddesses, talking about fierce warriors and wars conquered. After listening to these stories for two evenings baby Jesus doesn't like the stories anymore especially the heroes.

"He's not God," baby Jesus says after a story about Iris. "I know God," he declares, "And, he's none of these you call gods."

Everyone is amazed that such a small boy talks like that, but they don't like his argument about their gods. Baby Jesus proves them wrong the following day when they tell another story of another god of Egypt. He tells them the hero is not a god. He cast a stone away from him and speaks.

"I want a tree." Immediately a tree grows out of the ground and grows tall and large. "Can your gods do that?" He asks.

They marvel at him, and many kids fear him, saying he's a magician. Mary and Joseph keep watch on him and prevent him from joining in the story-telling session. Mary keeps him in the tent, telling him stories of the Israelites, starting from Abraham to Moses who received the Ten Commandments.

"All these you will learn before your thirteenth birthday, Isa," she tells him.

She's often left alone with him in the tent all day since Joseph gets a job in a furniture making company, making Egyptian furniture. He leaves the tent early and doesn't return until late in the evening. They live in the tent for two weeks before Joseph announces that he's found a house for them.

"We're moving into a house," he says.

"That's good," Mary says. "At least Isa will have his own room."

"That and a courtyard of our own," Joseph says.

When they reach the house, it turns out to be a small house compared to the large ones they see around them. However, Joseph and his friends from work have rebuilt it and turned it into a spacious living space with two bedrooms. They even have a fence around it, painted in white. Mary expresses emotion hugging Joseph and kissing him.

"It's beautiful," she says.

She's right. The house does look beautiful with a picket fence around it. From that day onward Mary makes the house as homely as possible. They live there for the next five months, leaving two weeks before baby Jesus's third birthday.

The event leading to their leaving Dairout is symbolic. After his bold declaration to the Egyptians, that their gods are not God, baby Jesus seems to have grown much more quickly. Mary's stories of the Israelites and their departure from Egypt under God's mighty hand, strengthen his courage. When they move into their house. Joseph returns to work and Mary and baby Jesus stay at home. On occasions they will walk into the city and do some shopping. During one shopping trip, while Mary is busy bargaining with the stall keeper, baby Jesus wanders away from her. He has locked eyes with a boy sitting on the floor across the stall. The boy is paralyzed and looks ridiculously small with both legs folded under him. Baby Jesus gradually moves closer to him. He reaches him and speaks.

129

"Would you like to walk?"

"I've never walked since I was born," the boy says looking at baby Jesus curiously.

"Believe me. You can walk," baby Jesus says. "Get up and walk."

The boy looks confused.

"How?" He asks.

"Stretch your legs out and stand up," baby Jesus says.

The kid does just that. Little by little his two legs stretch out before him, then he lifts himself from the ground and stands on his two feet. He looks at baby Jesus, surprise on his face. The people around see him jump up. He couldn't be more than twelve years old but where the paralysis affects him, he looks small. Standing, he looks strong again and his face is all smiles. Mary grabs baby Jesus.

"Don't be talking to strangers, Isa," she says.

The boy grabs her by the hand and speaks.

"Sorry Ma. Is he your son? He just healed me."

"Please, young man. Don't say that to people," Mary says softly, moving closer to the boy. But people are watching them even though some still look clueless.

"What should I tell people when they ask me?"

"Tell them Jesus healed you," says baby Jesus as Mary pulls him away.

The crowd is growing, with people asking.

"What's going on?" "What happened?"

When Joseph returns from work, Mary told him what happened in the city. She explains what she said to the boy, how she asked him to keep it quiet.

"I don't think he will," Joseph says. "You know people. They talk."

"What are we going to do?" Mary asks. "They might find us again."

"It's always something with this your son, Mary," Joseph says. "He's always up to something."

"He's God's son, Joseph," Mary says simply.

"I guess we have to wait and see if this boy keeps his word," Joseph says.

"Are you putting our safety in the hands of one boy?"

"No Mary. Of course not. I'm just saying we can stay here for some time till we really need to go."

As the days turn into months it appears the boy did keep his mouth shut. But three months after the incident, the boy meets Mary and baby Jesus in the city again. He recognizes them and introduces himself.

"What did you want now?" Mary says.

"I just want to say thank you to your son again," he says and introduces his family to them.

His father, mother, sisters and brothers, are all there. They all come around them and praise baby Jesus. Mary wants to leave but they walk her back home. This way, they learn where they live. Mary blames herself for leading them back to the house. She tells Joseph and he speaks.

"Nothing might come out of it. They're just a normal happy family."

But Mary is worried, and her worry doesn't go away as the days unfold. The next day the boy comes with two of his friends and plays with baby Jesus in their courtyard. He says his name is Ahmed and he'd never walked since he was born.

"He's really a lovely boy." Mary says to Joseph later in the night. "He plays with Isa and even helps me draw water from the well. I'm just worried if people get to know us."

131

"When that comes, we'll deal with it." Joseph says. "The Lord is on our side. Don't be afraid."

Mary does just that. She decides to let go of her worries and give baby Jesus space to express himself. She allows him to walk around the courtyard with Ahmed and his friends. Baby Jesus sits with the older boys and talks to them.

"Why do you worry for?" He says. "Look at the birds of the air. They have no homes, sown not and do not gather but they're fed. God can do more for you a man than for the birds."

"How do you know about God? You're just too young to know who's God and who's not," Ahmed says. "In Egypt we worship men as gods. Our pharaoh is a god in his own class."

"They all die and fade away," baby Jesus says. "God never dies or fades away."

Everyday Ahmed comes and sits with baby Jesus and plays with him. He seems to have an affection for baby Jesus after he'd healed his paralysis. But as soon as one of Mary's worries goes away another comes in its place.

It is a holiday when Mary, baby Jesus and Joseph walk into the city. Somehow Ahmed finds them among the throng of people walking the street. He sits outside a shop with his friends talking and playing when Mary and Joseph and baby Jesus walk by. They enter a butcher shop and Mary and Joseph concentrate on bargaining with the butcher.

Baby Jesus walks out of the shop either to meet Ahmed outside or for something else, the instance he walks out a hand grabs him. Two tall men grab baby Jesus and runs down the street with him. Ahmed and his friend see it.

"Hey stop," Ahmed shouts.

The men don't stop. They run down the street. Ahmed's

friends give them a chase, while Ahmed runs into the shop to alert Mary and Joseph.

"They've taken your son," he shouts.

"Who? Isa," Mary shouts, turning away from the butcher.

"Yes, Isa. Jesus. They've taken him," Ahmed says.

Joseph runs down the road with Mary after him. The men can be seen running ahead of them. Ahmed's friends are behind the men while Ahmed races past all of them. The men breach a corner into another street and head into the desert.

Another man waits at the edge of the desert with a camel for them. He's urging them to hurry. Ahmed catches up with them before they can reach their camel. He jumps from behind, landing on the one man who has baby Jesus on his shoulder. The man falls forward and baby Jesus lands on the ground along with Ahmed. The other man grabs Ahmed and speaks.

"You'll pay for this, you little street rat."

Meanwhile, baby Jesus runs down the street to meet Joseph who is catching up with them. Ahmed's friends launch an attack at the two men especially the one who has Ahmed by the neck. They free Ahmed from his grasp and set about beating both men.

Joseph arrives with baby Jesus in his arm. He can see that the two men are Jews and Herod's men. Joseph is so infuriated with himself for letting his guard down. When Mary reaches them, he says.

"Mary, I'm so sorry. I let my guard down."

"Not your fault. I did as well. We have Ahmed to thank."

They return home and Joseph sets about packing their things.

"We're leaving," he says. "We'll go down south."

"But, Joseph, we've nearly gone through Egypt."

"Have faith," he says.

They leave the city of Dairout and head south on their camel. They do have some things in their favour. Joseph has lots of money on him and they can support themselves for the journey.

∽ Chapter 20 ∾

BROKEN IDOLS

After leaving the city of Dairout, the holy family sets forth on a southernly path. Going through the desert, down and down they go. The bluster of heat of the southern part of Egypt thrashes against them yet it doesn't dwindle their effort.

Baby Jesus is still affected by what happened in Dairout because all day, until their rest for the night he says nothing. He's just absorbed within himself not eating or talking to his mother or anyone they meet along the way. They pitch their tent for the night and it's then that baby Jesus comes out of his shell.

"Mama, why does these men carry me away from you?" He asks.

Mary feels a pinch in her heart. It's like a needle prick and she aches for affection. She hugs him and says, "Isa, these men work for a bad man. They want to take you to him and he's going to kill you."

"Why? What did I do wrong?"

"You did nothing wrong but to exist," she says. "He's the king and wants to kill you because he knows you're going to become a king in his place." She tells him of his birth and God's promise that he will free his people. Then, she says. "You see Isa, it's your destiny to become king of the Jews and free them from bad kings."

"Mama, I don't want to be a king anymore."

"Why Isa?" she asks. "Being a king is the best thing you can do for the Jews."

"No mama. I can't share a position with a bad man. I will think of other ways."

She lays him to sleep and goes outside the tent where Joseph sits.

"Isa said he doesn't want to be a king anymore."

"Why? What changed his mind?"

"I think it's Herod," she says.

They said nothing further on the matter, but Mary never stops thinking about it. And the more she thinks about it, the more she understands her son's decision. She reasoned that he must see the throne as a corrupt position if a bad man is on it. She silently curses Herod for taking away her son's destiny.

However, by the morning she has resolve and hands everything to God. Saying her prayers silently in her heart as they embark back on their journey. Baby Jesus as well seems to have resolved the issue within himself. For the rest of the journey, he listens and talks to his mother as she tells him more stories. They sing songs to warm up their spirit on the journey. They try not think of the hazards along the way, with the boiling heat of the desert sun beating down hard on them.

They appear to be in oneness of spirit for the journey until they arrive at Qoussia. This is a small city close to the Nile. On reaching the city, the holy family is glad to enter a city so soon and happily in hope to find a home there. There's nothing at the entrance into the city to tell of the hideous idols they hide within. Being strangers, the holy family can't tell until they reach the heart of the city and discover an array of idols laying around with worshippers beneath them bowing down to earth. On seeing this Joseph stops.

"Why are you stopping?" Mary asks.

"Look ahead," he says. "What can you see?"

When Mary sees what Joseph sees she tries to avoid baby Jesus from seeing it.

"Isa please close your eyes as we go through here."

But as she says that she can see people running heltter-skeltter from the idols. She watches the array of twelve or more idols blast off into the air shattering into pieces. Mary looks at her son.

"You've seen them."

"They're fools," baby Jesus says.

"Joseph, we can't stay in this city," Mary says. "Please let's go through and find some other city to stay."

Without another word Joseph resumes his walk. As they continue more idols along the road are falling and smashing into pieces. The people are confused, they can't tell what's happening. They don't accuse the holy family since they're just walking through, and they don't have any weapons to smash their idols.

Joseph just walks on. As they walk more idols fall until they exit the city at the southern end. They walk out of the city and continue their journey.

Baby Jesus doesn't say another word about the city of Qoussia or the people. Mary wants to know more about how her son thinks. On their next stop for the night, she talks to him just before she puts him to bed.

"Why are these people worshipping idols, fools, Isa?" She asks.

"God is not an idol. He's a living God," he says then looks

into her eyes. "Mama, these idols have no life in them, and they who have life in them bow to them."

Mary is amazed at his understanding and says.

"It can only be God who teaches you."

Chapter 21

THIRD BIRTHDAY

They arrive in the city of Meir in the evening. The city is small compared to the cities they've gone through in the past. The people of Meir seem ordinary without any design to them, just like their houses which are spaced equally apart.

The courtyard of each house has an alleyway on the side before the next house and it continues, with the houses going around a large pyramid. Every alleyway leads to the pyramid. The residents appear to be pyramid builders, mostly because of small pyramids on the edge of the city. Some of them move around but the people that make Meir their home trade in goods and farming.

After going through the city for hours. Mary and Joseph are sure the city is safe and hospitable. They even find a house from a shopkeeper who introduces himself as Hudini. Joseph walks into his shop to buy baby Jesus a drink and then asks.

"Would you know where we can find a place to stay?"

"How many of you?" Hudini asks.

"Oh, just me and my wife and our son," Joseph says. "He's turning three in a week, and we want a place where we can celebrate his birthday."

"That's okay. It just happens that I have a room," he says. "It's a small room, but I guess if you're doing a celebration, it won't be big enough for many people."

"Oh, on that," says Joseph. "We're not expecting too many people. We'll take your room."

The rent is low, just ten debens. He pays for a week and then says.

"I would pay you a week at a time."

"That's just okay with me," Hudini says and then walks them round to the house which is at the back of the shop.

It opens to another road and across the road is a forest. Baby Jesus often comes out to play on the road, standing at the edge of the road and watching the forest. He grew awareness of the forest life by watching what goes on from the road, watching the birds lift off the trees and land again without any trouble to the trees. He watches and considers nature.

Joseph on the other hand, tries to get a job but for a week he can't find anything, and almost gives up until the shop keeper, Hudini sees what he made for their house.

He sees him making stuff in the small back garden of the house and approaches Joseph.

"These are lovely items you're making here," he says. "How do you learn this craft?"

Joseph explains to him that he learnt the craft when he was just a teenager and had worked in many different places in Egypt as a craftsman. Hudini is interested and works out a trade with Joseph. He says he will make space in his shop for the things Joseph makes and he can sell them on commission. They both agree on a deal and Joseph is happy to work and make things.

The furniture he makes are a mixture of both Jewish and Egyptian styles. The people love his pieces. Within the first week

140

Joseph is making money. When the week ends and it's time for baby Jesus's third birthday, they've got everything ready.

They didn't expect to have a visitor, but someone did visit them on the day. It's early evening and Joseph is in the backyard making furniture. The family plans to come in later and sit down and have a meal together to mark baby Jesus's third birthday.

Mary has been cooking through the day and baby Jesus is only glad to help, picking this and bringing that.

As the evening comes, they're ready to go in when three men walk in from the street. Behind them are two more all looking misgiving except for the one leading them smiling. He comes in and introduces himself to Mary.

"Good evening, Mary," he says. "My name is Godwin. I'm sure we've met before. Do you remember the foreign affairs minister for Judea?"

Mary does remember. She was wondering where she'd seen his face before. When he says it, she freezes and the dish in her hand drops, the food splatting on the floor.

Baby Jesus is in the room sitting with a plate of food in front of him. He comes into the hallway where he finds the men with his mother. He sees that his mother looks frightened although she doesn't scream.

"Hey young one," says Godwin, seeing baby Jesus. "I've come for you."

Mary runs to her child. She hugs him and calls out.

"Joseph, there are people in the house. Help."

Two men immediately walk towards Joseph who is coming in from the back of the house and grab him. Joseph doesn't struggle, letting them lead him to the room.

Godwin is sitting on a chair while they've got Mary tied to another chair. Baby Jesus is standing in the middle of the room watching what's going on. Joseph can't go to him because the two men hold him back. They lead him to a chair and tie him down. Godwin turns to baby Jesus.

"I'm told you can do miracles. I've been following your record all over Egypt's cities. You've been leaving your mark. And, I thought to myself, you'll soon get through Egypt then what? Where else would you go? So, I've come to solve that problem for you by leading you back to Judea myself." He laughs heartily then adds. "I'm not looking for your approval or your parents. The king wants to see you and that's my job to deliver you to him."

"Why does the king want me?" Baby Jesus asks.

Godwin smiles ruefully, he tries to avoid baby Jesus's gaze, but baby Jesus locks eyes with him.

"You don't want to tell me that the king wants to kill me," he says looking straight into Godwin's eyes. "But I know. It's written all over you. You work for a bad man, and you don't like it. You're afraid for your own life."

"All right, shut up," Godwin yells. "So, you can psyche me out. Is that one of your gifts as well, holy child?"

"Will you kill a soul that sin not?" baby Jesus asks Godwin.

"Look, it's not my decision. The king decides. He says and I do."

"I'm not a slave to a wicked man. Let's go to him," baby Jesus says.

Mary screams, and Hudini hears her in his shop. He runs round to their room, and is confronted by the men. He runs back after seeing what's going on. One man among them tries to give him a chase, but Godwin calls him back.

"What we need to do is get out of here. Leave that man alone."

"What are we doing with the mother and father?" One of the men ask.

"Leave them tied down here," Godwin says. "That will give us time to get far."

They hold baby Jesus and set out of the room. Mary is screaming in agony.

"My son, God where are you? Somebody please, help. They're taking my son away."

Nobody seems to hear Mary's pleading while the men walk away with baby Jesus. They reach the front section of the house which looks towards the forest and stops.

Outside the house there, a large crowd from the neighbourhood has gathered. Lots of men jump on Godwin and his men as Hudini points them out. They grab Godwin and his four men and walk them towards the forest. As they lead them away baby Jesus walks back inside to find Hudini untying his mother and Joseph. He runs to his mother and hugs her.

Meanwhile, as the crowd are leading Godwin and his men towards the forest, one of Godwin's men breaks into a run and dashes away into the forest. The crowd keeps a hold on Godwin and the others. They lead them into the forest and tie them to a tree and leave them there. Then the crowd gathers around the holy family and comforts them.

As soon as the crowd goes away Joseph gathers his family and tells them they must leave the city. Mary agrees with him, and they pack up. In the night they leave the city and make their way southward.

Mary knows without any doubt that her son won't want to be

a king. The throne is corrupt, and Jesus won't want a thing to do with it.

"Why should I stand where a wicked man stands?" She remembers.

Chapter 22

HEROD'S DEATH

King Herod has been on his sick bed for nearly a year now. Not that he can't do anything, because he still attends his councils. His problem is his swelling penis and the pus. Having sought many medical attentions, he resorts to attempting suicide. He can't mate with a woman anymore, and the itching and light pains he gets from it feel so uncomfortable. His suicide attempt is prompted by his wife, Herodine.

"You're not worthy of being a king of the Jews," she says. "In fact, you're not a man."

"You can say that now," says Herod. "This illness will go away, and the women of Judea will know who's a man."

They're in their bedroom and Herod as usual, is scratching his penis. The instant he sees pus, he screams.

"Damn you, Herod," says Herodine. "You've been cursed."

"Who dares curse a king?" Says Herod still in pain.

"I don't know, probably the gods."

"Don't you joke," says Herod, looking around his room.

He suddenly remembers what the spirit of the young king told him. He screams again in agony, and Herodine runs out of the chamber to find help. She returns with a maid. When Herod sees her, he yells.

"Stay away from me."

The maid leaves the room because as all of them know, it might be her death if she remains. After nearly a year he's fed up and wants to die. His wife hands him a potion.

"Try this," she says, giving him a small jar.

"What's in it?"

"I don't know. It either heals you or kills you," she replies.

"I will take both," Herod replies and takes the jar.

He gulps down the contents and expects to die or get better, but after several days neither has happened. It's not clear if Herodine wants to help the king to a merciful death. However, it doesn't work, and Herod remains in his room since his illness get worse.

"You can't even come up with a good poison," he says to his wife.

"That's what they gave me."

"Was that supposed to kill me?"

"Nobody wants to kill you, Herod," she says. She looks at him and winches. "It's just a disgrace to see you like this."

"Anyway, I've made my last demand. And you get nothing."

"You cruel man. Haven't I served you, long enough? Even when you can't make me a woman."

"Well, you can marry the next king. That will be a reward to you."

She wants to club him to death, but she quietly walks out of the room. She'd learned long ago that living with Herod is fettered with fear.

Herod can still hear the cries of babies. He looks around when he hears the cries again. Then, he rises from his bed and curses heaven.

Herodine doesn't sleep in the bedroom with Herod. She

sleeps in another chamber in the house. She is thinking of her next life. What will happen to her after Herod's death? She somehow knows after several months of the same illness that he won't make it out alive. She's given up on him. Death is better than shame.

In the middle of the night, Herod screams loudly. He is in immense pain from his penis. Herodine runs into the room. He looks pale and struggles to talk. He says nothing to her but winches in pain.

"You brought this on yourself," she says.

"Get lost, you whore," Herod screams at her.

She goes back to her room and sleeps. In the morning she hears nothing from Herod and goes into the room to check on him. King Herod lies on his bed with eyes wide open and his penis in his hand. She first thinks he's playing with it, but after moving closer to the bed she discovers that he's dead. The pus the penis made is all over the bedsheet, leaving white stains.

She rushes out of the room and calls the maids and palace officials. One of the council men, orders the maids to clothe him and cover his wound. Afterward, they pronounce King Herod dead of natural causes. He's about sixty- nine years old, not old enough to die of natural causes.

The whole of Judea mourns the loss of their king, and all his allies around the world are informed. When they wash his dead body for burial, they see his penis is huge, and still making pus. From the morgue the rumour starts to spread that King Herod died of gonorrhoea.

Chapter 23

THE VISITATION

After leaving Meir behind, the holy family journeys southward again, all moody and exhausted. They have one thing
going through their mind, and that's the madness at Meir.

Mary can't wrap her mind around it. She's filled with what ifs.
What if the people hadn't come to their aid? What if, is all she
can say for a long while until they stop for the night. Then she
wants to know why baby Jesus decided to go with the men. She
thinks its rather a strong decision for a three-year-old to make.

Joseph hasn't lost all thought. He'd packed most of the food
Mary prepared for baby Jesus's third birthday. They get to eat
that on their night stopover. Mary still looks lost and wounded
emotionally. She eats little and so does baby Jesus. Before she
puts him to bed, she asks.

"Isa, would you have gone with those wicked men, knowing
they we're going to kill you?"

"Mama, I have nothing to fear. Knowing they are the reason
we're running around is not good. So, if they take me to the
wicked king, they can; if he wants to kill me, he can try."

"Not even death?" She asks. "You will lose Mama and Joseph
forever. Because the king can really kill you. He's wicked."

"Is that why you fear the king?" Baby Jesus says. "But, killing he can kill, he can't make alive. He has no life in him."

She doesn't know what to say so she kisses him on the forehead.

"Get some sleep, Isa. We still have a long way to go in the morning."

Baby Jesus closes his eyes and sleeps while Mary and Joseph sit up talking, that it could happen again. From the way Joseph sees it, even though the people helped them, they were still attacked, and it could happen again.

"I'm sorry. I can't protect you, Mary," he says.

"Don't be stupid," Mary says. "There's absolutely nothing you could've done there. There were five of them and one of you."

It's true Joseph feels useless and sad about the whole thing. He's been wishing and wishing upon wishing that he had great powers to fight them away. But he knows nothing comes out of wishes. So, apologizing to Mary for his insufficiency is the only proper thing he can do at the moment.

Mary, on the other hand, saw it coming because she's been watching him all along, even though she's been absorbed in her own thoughts. In fact, she's noticed the quietness they all showed on the journey.

"I feel so useless," Joseph says. "They could've walked away into the desert with Isa."

"I know," she replies. "The Lord is our shepherd."

"We don't need to be afraid, do we?"

"Absolutely not."

They later go in and sleep waking up early and proceeding on their journey. They walk the whole day in the scorching sun, reaching the town of Gabal Qussqam, later in the evening.

Gabal Qussqam is a small settlement with a governor, but

when the holy family reaches this settlement in the desert, they can't find a place to stay. They eventually resort to sleeping in a cave.

"Let's stay in the cave for the night and by tomorrow we can find a house," Joseph says.

Mary doesn't argue, and they make their home in a cave at the base of a mountain for the night. By morning, Mary has a complete change of heart.

"Why don't we stay in the cave? It's safer here than in a house, I think," she says.

Joseph considers their options, thinking that being in the cave will save them rent money. He's worried about the comfort of the cave at the same time. And, he worries about their safety if Herod's men find them there. Surely, they won't have any help.

On the other hand, Herod's men will probably be searching in town and not in the mountains and caves. They've been safe in caves, the past few years. So, he agrees with her. Joseph starts making the cave homely for them. He builds a bed for them and a small bed for baby Jesus. Baby Jesus gives them water from a spring on the side of the mountain. He realizes they need water and walks to the mountain side, where he makes a spring flow.

"Mama, we need water. I will bring a spring," he says, before he walks out of the cave.

"I know he's God among us," Mary says to herself afterward.

Joseph decides what he can do is to make stuff. He sets about making small furniture and ornaments which he then loads on to the camel and takes into town to sell. He gets the idea when they walk into town to buy provisions and he sees a furniture shop. He asks them for work, but they don't want him. So, he decides to make do on his own. He sets his furniture up by the roadside and sells the pieces there.

150

At times he's gone for most of the day which leaves Mary and baby Jesus alone in the cave. But Joseph always finds his way back at night. They stay in the cave for months living freely off the wild at most times. Baby Jesus has surely forgotten the last kidnapping attempt because he plays well with his mother and laughs at her jokes.

The best things he does is to doodle on the ground with a stick. He draws things on the ground and leaves them there or at times calls his mother to come and see what he's drawn. Mary's home teaching changes over the months. Since they have nothing to do all day, she lets him do what he does which is to draw on the ground. She teaches him the Aramaic alphabet she knows and many more things. Baby Jesus has a sharp mind, as soon as she shows him something, he knows it and draws it on his own.

Meanwhile, on his daily runs into town for sales, Joseph has managed to find out more about the town and its surroundings. One night when he comes back, he tells Mary.

"There's only one city left in Egypt we haven't been to."

"Must we go there?" Mary asks, thinking ahead.

"People told me, it's a beautiful city. It's on the edge of the Nile right down south."

"Why are you telling me this?" Mary asks.

"I thought we could go there and leave this cave. We'll find a house there to live."

"But I feel safe here," says Mary. "I like how close we are to nature. Me and Isa climb up the mountain and we often walk around in the woods. I like nature."

"But we're living in a cave when there're houses around," Joseph says.

"Joseph, it's not about where we live. It's about where we find peace. It's very peaceful here."

151

They remain in the cave, but Joseph continues to suggest that they leave. Mary refuses each time. Eventually, Joseph doesn't ask anymore, then they've been there for five months.

The following month goes easily without Joseph questioning Mary's decision anymore. He adjusts himself to living in the cave. However, when they've been there for six months, Joseph has a dream.

Baby Jesus is three and half years old when Mary tells Joseph that she's pregnant with his baby. The joy in him is blinding that he lifts baby Jesus up in the air throwing him up several times and hugging Mary.

"You're going to be a big brother," Joseph says.

He's not sure if baby Jesus knows what that means, so he says.

"Your mother is pregnant. She's going to have a baby."

That does shock baby Jesus, and he asks his mother.

"Mother, are you having a baby."

"Not just yet, Isa, but very soon," she says.

Joseph is very happy as he lies down to sleep that night. Deep in his sleep, in the middle of the night, an angel of the Lord visits them in the cave. In Joseph's dream the angel touches him to wake him up.

"Blessed Joseph. Take the child and his mother and return into Israel for those who seek the child's life are dead."

Joseph awakes from his sleep immediately and wakes Mary. He tells her his dream and what the angel said.

"That means Herod and his men are dead," Mary says.

"It might just be Herod alone," says Joseph. "They all do his wishes but take away the head and the body will fall."

"What about? . . . What's his name again?" Mary says. "I mean the foreign minister."

"You mean Godwin."

"Yes. What about him? Won't he still want my son?"

"For what? He's only doing Herod's wishes. But when Herod dies so do all his wishes."

Mary still looks worried. And Joseph seeing this says.

"Mary, there's absolutely nothing left to be afraid or worried about anymore. We've won. We're free. We can return home now."

"I still find it hard to believe," Mary says. "Just like that everything is over."

"Yes. I guess so," Joseph says.

They start preparing for their departure. They wake baby Jesus up in the morning and tell him the good news. Mary says.

"Isa, we can go back home now."

"Where?" baby Jesus asks. He is not sure where home is exactly.

Mary has told him many times where home is but having lived in so many places he can't grasp where she means by home. So, she says aloud.

"Isa, we're going home to Israel."

Baby Jesus doesn't look at all pleased, just accepting.

"When do we leave?" He asks.

"Today. Now. As soon as we finish."

Before they can finish packing up Joseph has a plan for their return journey.

"We have to go into Assuit to get the boat up the river till we can get a boat to Galilee."

"You mean the city you've always wanted to go?" Mary says.

"What harm is in it?" Joseph says. "It's the last city we haven't been to. Why not and make our way home from there? We'll take a boat. I have money on me, lots of it."

Mary in her happy mood can't resist him, so she shrugs her shoulders.

"If we must go, then let's go," she says.

Then as Joseph is packing their stuff on to the camel she says.

"Just to make this clear. I'm only going because you've been bugging me about it."

They set forth and journey into Assuit at the south end of Egypt where they catch a boat up the river. Assuit is a small city just growing. They mostly farm and do some fishing.

The holy family doesn't stay in the city but catches a boat going up the Nile. They set forth on their way back into Israel and then Nazareth, where Jesus grows up.

The End

Author Note

Thank you for purchasing this book and reading it to the end. Just to let you know that although this story is all imagination, it wasn't written without the consent of the Lord and the help of the Spirits. When I conceived the idea for this story I said to the Lord.

> "Lord, I have a story about you, and
> I think I should be the one that writes it."

Then, I went to my desk to structure it. I was thinking of one story, but I end up with three stories and more afterward. This is the first book, Jesus the toddler years is on the way then it's Jesus in high school.

I appreciate the benefit of the lord's grace that he grants me to be able to write this story. It's by his grace alone that we live. And that same grace extends to you through our lord Jesus Christ.

Thank you and God bless.

Author Bio

I was born in Lagos Nigeria, west Africa in December 18, 1973. I am the first child of my parent, three brothers and one sister. From an early age, my mother had always advices me to draw closer to God. I did my baptism when I was eighteen years old before I travelled abroad.

I came to the UK in 1995, and since then I have been living in England, UK. I am now blessed with four children and four step-sons. Their daily growing up is my main motivation because I think about what they can learn from me and what I can impact on them.

You can get to know more about me and my work on my website.

www.femimartin.co.uk

Visit and subscribe to get to know about my new books. You can also join me on Twitter, facebook and Instagram

Milton Keynes UK
Ingram Content Group UK Ltd.
UKHW011820170823
427026UK00001B/80

9 798223 044406